True to Her Herself

Barbara M Webb

Cover Design by Mirna Gilman, Books Go Social

Acknowledgements

Thanks to Dayanara Pazos, superb International chef, for her advice regarding capitalisation of names of dishes and wines.

Contents

Chapter 1

Moira thrust the key into the door. It glided in but wouldn't turn. The door was unlocked. Strange. She had left for school after Guido that morning as he had to visit a client in the south of Sydney at 8:30 am. Had she been careless?

The newspaper publicity for recent robberies in the area flashed through her head. Perhaps she had better enter their apartment with a neighbour. Moira knocked on Martin's door, hoping it was his day off work.

"Martin, could you come and check my apartment with me please? The door is unlocked. I'm worried an intruder may have…"

"No problem."

His solid, bulky, frame led the way. Moira crept in behind him. They both hesitated on the threshold. Moira allowed the utter silence to seep into her. She could almost hear her pounding heart. Her throat was dry. The two rooms on the right were open and Martin checked each one in turn. Moira held her breath.

Better let him handle the situation. A muffled chortle emerged from the bedroom. Startled, she jumped. Martin stormed towards the closed door, pushed it open, then came to a sudden halt. He thrust his right arm out as if to stop Moira entering the room.

"What the hell are you doing here?" a voice growled.

Moira recognised Guido's voice. Feeling drops of sweat roll down her back, she clasped her hand to her mouth. It was then that she caught sight of her naked husband in bed with a woman. She gasped. Guido eventually noticed her. She felt as if she was floating, as if she had left her body. It was all so surreal.

"So you have a boyfriend too?" Guido sneered, his lips curling. The cheek of him. The woman was struggling to cover herself with the sheet. Fuelled by a spasm of rage, Moira sprinted in the direction of the woman and tore at the sheet with both hands, shouting, "Get out of my home!"

The young woman, poised by now, surveyed Moira up and down, and eased herself out of bed, the sheet still wrapped around her.

"Get out," Moira hissed. Anger flooded her.

Guido had the decency to put his boxer shorts on. As Moira stepped backwards, she nearly tripped over the empty champagne bottle on the floor. Emboldened by Martin's presence, she kicked the bottle, out of frustration. Her face and neck had turned red and she spat out the words, "Guido Capaldi, you are despicable."

Betrayal of the worst kind. In her bed. Enough was enough.

Aware of her embarrassment and humiliation, Martin sneaked out of the bedroom but hovered by the front door. Guido ignored Moira, entered the en-suite and banged the door shut. She flung the wardrobe open, reached for her weekend bag and rammed random clothes in. Her hands were shaking.

Moira flounced out of the bedroom, scooping up her handbag. She saw her reflection in the mirror in the hallway. Red blotches covered her face and neck. Was that really her? Hating herself for losing her cool, she hurried out of the front door as if hoping to leave the pain behind.

She tried to simmer down. Only an hour and a half at her school to go, and then it would be holiday time. She clambered in the car. Should she be driving? To hell with being careful. Bristling with resentment, she had enough self-control to ring a few of the women in her social set and challenge them with the question that was uppermost in her mind.

"How long has Guido been having an affair?"

The embarrassed silences spoke for themselves.

"Maybe four months," was the most common reply. Mortified, she longed to escape from her humiliation and calm her whirling thoughts.

Today was the last day of the spring term in 1985. All the staff were suffering from stress at the end of term with examinations, assessments and reports. A bad time for personal problems to surface. How extraordinary that she had discovered Guido's infidelity on the one day she chose to lunch at home.

That morning, the staff had had to attend an extra meeting. The air in the staffroom had felt oppressive, despite the windows being open, and

Moira had been struggling with the start of a migraine. She rarely went home for lunch but she had slipped out of the staffroom and headed for the car park, where she had found her car like an oven. It would have been possible to fry an egg on the bonnet, despite it being April.

Five minutes later she had turned her car into the garage belonging to the apartments. After parking her car, she had taken the lift to their penthouse. Salad and ham were what she had had in mind. Her husband's infidelity was what she had encountered.

Moira disliked her emotional reaction in the apartment. It made her feel that she was just like Guido in her loss of control. She checked into a hotel for the weekend, at Bondi, well away from her home in Bronte. The royal blue sea sparkled outside but she curled herself into a foetal position on the bed. Tears rained on to the pillow. Her heart constricted with the pain of betrayal. Getting up in an effort to shower and dress, she would turn round and just slink back into bed. Then it was easy to slip into a darkness that had no defined hours. Drifting in and out of sleep most of the time, Moira was unaware of Friday and Saturday passing. Meals were an irrelevance.

On the Sunday, Moira gaped at herself in the bathroom mirror. She saw the doleful eyes in the hollowed out face. She felt light-headed and giddy. When was the last time she had eaten? She sat down on the bed. Moira admonished herself for her emotional reaction, as if that would obliterate her rawness. Was any man worth this pain? What was done was done. It was time to address her needs, despite the rawness of her feelings. Staying at a hotel in the expensive eastern suburbs was not the answer.

Moira felt the need to spend time close to nature – somewhere far away. She called a friend who had a small beach house in Narrabeen on the North Shore.

"Stay as long as you want to," Joyce had said.

"Just till the end of next week would be fine," Moira replied.

In mid-April the sea temperatures were warm compared with October, which was the official start of the summer.

On Monday when Guido would be at work, Moira returned to the apartment and headed for the wardrobe in their bedroom. Her tongue stuck to the roof of her mouth and her stomach turned over. It was impossible not to feel that her home had been violated. Grabbing extra clothes, including shorts and tops she might need for the beach, she shoved everything into a suitcase.

Moira then wandered listlessly through the rooms, lost in her thoughts. Though Guido had contributed to housekeeping and spent money lavishly on social life, particularly in the early years of marriage, it was she who had organised the upgrading of the apartment. He avoided involvement in the process of homemaking. It was Moira who had collected furniture from garage sales and auctions, bought paintings and nurtured the house plants. Investing in extra garage space, paying all the bills, including the mortgage, became her responsibility. Surely she had been more than a meal ticket?

Finally Moira reached the lounge where three vases of roses stood bunched together on the coffee table with a card embossed with

Sorry I love ONLY you. You know that!

Guido's romantic gestures had always appealed to her in the past when they were an expression of his romantic love. Now they reminded her of his duplicity. The words seemed hollow. All she could feel was the emptiness that results from loss of trust.

Moira had no plans for her immediate future other than removing herself from Guido. To stop him trying to contact her, she wrote him a note to say she was visiting a former school friend in Queensland for the two weeks of the school holidays and left it on a table by the front door. How easily the lies slid off her pen.

Driving across the centre of the city in her Toyota Corolla Coupe, Moira headed for the North Shore. The Sydney Harbour Bridge was awash with traffic, honking cars working their way over the bridge like bustling ants. She was oblivious to the congestion; she concentrated on her driving. Normally she would have enjoyed the journey, particularly driving through the green belt of wooded and serene suburbs such as St Ives. Today, raw feelings replaced any pleasure she might have had.

At Narabeen, Moira stopped to buy supplies of salad items, water and fruit juices. After another half hour she reached the outskirts of civilisation and Joyce's property, thankful to have left her home suburb where she might have had to face Guido, other teachers, or students from school. The isolation of this beach cabin suited her. She was here to extend herself physically, to push her body to extremes, and to forget the turmoil of betrayal.

It was a typical Australian beach house with a weatherboard exterior, in a grassy space surrounded by eucalyptus trees giving it shaded coolness. A few hibiscus shrubs grew close to the house. Cane chairs stood on the roofed terrace in front, useful for an afternoon doze. The house had basic cooking facilities, a bathroom and an open plan living space. A spacious bedroom had been added as if an afterthought. A ten-minute walk led to the beach, which in no way resembled Bondi or the other beaches in the affluent eastern suburbs. Moira sat down to drink her mineral water before unpacking her swimsuits and towels.

She enjoyed the garden and its tranquillity which was better than the artificial peace of pools and cocktails at a hotel. It was Guido who loved crowds and city life. For her, nature was a source of peace, a balm to her emotions.

After unpacking her small suitcase, Moira donned swimwear, shorts and T-shirt and jogged to the beach. Every time the memories of last Friday fluttered inside her head and the sobs wracked her, she beat her feet into the sand with fury. Sprinting for miles, she hoped to slow down the milling thoughts that woke her in the night and harassed her during the day.

Further along the deserted beach, Moira took off her outer clothes and dumped them on the sand. Dashing into the sea, allowing the surf to thrust itself against her body, she battled with the pummelling waves, as if thrashing her anger against the waves eased her inner ache. Moira climbed out at last and allowed the sun to dry her off before returning to the patrolled part of the beach. It was irresponsible of her to enter the rolling waves away from the lifeguards but she felt like rebelling against all of life. So what if the jelly fish or sharks were a threat!

Moira lay down on her belly and took her time to inhale and exhale, yoga-style. The gritty sand clung to her bare skin. Unwanted thoughts still squeezed into her mind. Guido's choice of lover and venue had humiliated her. By choosing their apartment for his fun, it was as if Guido wanted to be discovered, wanted to hurt her. His affair had overturned everything she had accepted as normal in her life.

She recalled the time when she was selected by Qantas to be an air hostess. Before Jumbo Jets even existed, the international airport for Australia was Kingsford Smith Airport in Sydney. Leaving her family home in Adelaide, she had shared a flat with three other trainee hostesses in Sydney. When she met Guido in those heady air hostessing days, Sydney's cosmopolitan lifestyle marked it as the business and cultural capital of Australia.

In the early days of the marriage, Guido had demonstrated his wish to please Moira by making weekend breakfasts, and bringing her flowers at regular intervals. Many invitations on the dinner party circuit ensured they both enjoyed a full social life. These days they had their separate interests: cycling for Guido with all the social life that a sport entailed; painting was what Moira embraced in her spare time. Guido frequently left for work early. His training cut into the weekday evenings so they didn't see much of each other except at weekends. Sunday became the weekly ritual for going out to dinner, just the two of them, usually to an Asian restaurant. She couldn't believe what their marriage had been reduced to.

Of course Moira loved her apartment and living by the beach. Staring at the changing moods of the Pacific Ocean was a way of relaxing for her. She was lucky to have been appointed to a school near her home. And they were only five miles from the city centre of Sydney so events in the Opera House or art galleries were located at a comfortable distance away from home; one of the advantages of living in the

Eastern suburbs.

That evening Moira was drawn to the water. She sat on an outcrop of rocks at the edge of the sand.

When you are alone, miles away from all you know and love, that's when you find out who you are.

Where did those words come from?

The white breakers looked eerie in the darkness as they spattered into nothingness. She had been in the sea four times that day. It was as if the salt in the water was cleansing her internal wounds. Time did not exist.

Finally Moira got up, climbed over the rocks and returned to the cabin where she lit some hurricane lamps. She wasn't hungry but forced herself to eat, in between frequent yawns that beckoned her to bed.

The days repeated themselves. Moira persevered with her austere diet and frequent bathing. Her body set up its own pace of crying, sleeping and pondering. Frequent bathing in the sea began to lull her into sleeping more soundly. Had she had been able to accept that their separate lives were bound to end up in infidelity, perhaps the heartbreak would have been less. The real question was whether she still loved him.

Moira had lived in the bubble of teaching for years. By now routine had squashed the enthusiasm of her early years. Intense innovative projects at work, such as piloting learning programs, were exciting but had now lost their lustre for her. The reality was that the duties of her executive position now stultified her. It wasn't just end of term fatigue. Was Guido's betrayal uncovering more than a faltering relationship?

On the fifth day, Moira took notice of the kookaburras cackling at breakfast time, and smiled. Possums frequented the nearby woods and stirred the greenery with their movements. The sea breeze ruffled the leaves gently. As the heat grew, the cicadas joined the chorus of nature's sounds. She became aware of the intensity of the cobalt blue sky. The sea shimmied under the sun's rays, changing from silver grey to blue and back again. The last few days had relaxed her because she had allowed the days to unravel. Her back muscles no longer ached. The physical exercise had released the stress.

A handful of surfers were braving the high waves, which curled into themselves and broke over the sand, leaving a surface of shining meringue foam over the beach. She breathed in the salty air of the Pacific Ocean. Had she forgotten how to make music in her life? It was time for her to feel fun again.

Within seconds, Moira was gripped with desire for change. Maybe this affair, making a travesty of her marriage, was an opportunity in disguise.

Chapter 2

After reading Moira's note to say she would be away for two weeks, Guido occupied himself with extra training and more business meetings. He was used to Moira engaging with extracurricular activities at school. She left early in the morning to arrive at school around 8 am. There was no need for her to spend years of her extra time on work. No financial compensations were forthcoming. Other teachers were committed to child-rearing, so perhaps she volunteered for the extra-curricular activities. Maybe she felt the need to address the vacuum that having her own children might have filled. He'd never really thought about it. Well, it gave him a sense of freedom. When she went to Europe, plenty of friends invited him to dinner.

Images from the fateful Friday returned to him from time to time. How was he to know that Moira would return home for lunch on the last day of the school term? School matters took up a lot of her time. Sometimes they made him feel superfluous in the marriage.

In the early years of their marriage, she had seemed softer, less brittle, and wore the Qantas smile. He remembered her saying that air hostesses in training would be ticked off if they went past the Superintendent's office without a smile. Moira used to bring some panache to their early dinner parties, with exotic dishes. Now she churned out cooked meals and stored them in the freezer so he could reheat his meals after training. Moira's single-minded focus on teaching goals had replaced the socialising of their early years together.

Guido still felt the effects of the recent shock of Moira discovering him with Rebecca in their home. He knew that some of the male partners, in the so-called happily married couples that they counted as their friends, strayed on occasion. What irked him like a stray stone in a shoe, was that Moira had been separating herself from him. There had been no sex for a couple of years, and not for want of him trying. Moira just seemed to clam up.

Rebecca had kissed him under the mistletoe last

Christmas at the office party. What started off as a social kiss ended up as a passionate exchange. The sensory vibrations had electrified him. When he arrived at the office the following Monday, he was aware of Rebecca's eyes boring into his back. He had to stay in the office till late finishing reports. When walking out of his office, he noticed Rebecca still working on files.

"Good night. Don't work too hard."

She peered coyly from beneath a wall of hair. He was mesmerized by the sheer physicality of her presence. That was four months ago.

Under the pretext of extra cycling training sessions, Guido began to meet her in her apartment, and sometimes in a hotel. Sex became an addiction for him, especially when Rebecca switched roles between the *vulnerable little girl* and the *seductress* who initiated sex. He found the contrast between the two roles erotic. She would hold his member in her delicate little hand, bringing about instant hardening. A few weeks into the affair, he told her he was married so there was no future for her. If anything, that encouraged her more. She was the instigator of the relationship with her frequent, "When shall we meet again?"

Working with her in the same company, Guido was unable to hide from the ever-present physical attraction he felt for her, and she knew how to draw him under her spell. When she told him she loved him and demanded more of his time, he realised he was losing control of the situation. Guido remembered how distorted and ugly Rebecca's face became when she was denied what she wanted.

On that fateful Friday, Rebecca had landed on his apartment doorstep uninvited; not that any of that excused his stupidity in taking her to his marital bed once she was there. He puzzled over how she could have known he was at home on that day? Rebecca must have stalked him. Then he remembered he had rung the office to say he was sick that morning; no doubt the office grapevine had been at work. A cooling-off period of distancing himself from her would be required, preferably before his next week-long business trip to Armidale and the north of

New South Wales.

Guido convinced himself he had not intended to humiliate Moira. They had hit bad patches in their marriage before and survived them. He hoped his gesture of buying roses would help to pacify her. Working in the sales department of an air conditioning company bored him, but at least he earned some income until he was ready to start up in business again. He felt guilty that he hadn't revealed the full extent of his debts to Moira.

When Guido returned home to find Moira's postcard with the message that she would be visiting friends for the two weeks of her school holidays, he was relieved not to have to face her just yet.

After cycling training, he joined his mates for a beer at the local pub. A few more pints later he was feeling more relaxed. Recently, the debts he had incurred in his last business were weighing him down, stressing him out. The conversation veered to the hike in Sydney property prices.

"You'd get a really good price for your apartment these days, mate," said a cyclist who happened to be an estate agent as well.

He was startled by the news. "Are you suggesting I should sell now?"

"It's up to you, mate. I can put you on to a friend if you're interested."

Now that the week at the beach was ending, Moira wanted to reconnect with her art class which she had neglected because of the school examination marking load. Her intention was to drive to the studio which was situated in the Rocks area of Sydney, and perhaps spend the rest of the weekend with Liz. Meeting Guido was not an option and she wanted to preserve the tranquillity that was now part of her.

Moira rang Liz that evening and touched upon events of the last week, without revealing too much at this stage.

"You can stay with me as long as you need to," said Liz.

At the studio, her thoughts drifted to her summer school holidays the previous December and January. She had left behind the heat and the beaches of the Australian summer, preferring to face frequent winter deluges while scouring the art galleries in Europe, studying the paintings she had come across between the covers of books in the History of Art course.

Her gaze fell on the easel drawing in front of her. The proportions were wrong; the head was too small for the body. That was the problem with longer studies. Her temperament was more suited to one- and five-minute sketches rather than hour-long studies. Concentrating was beyond her at the moment. She looked up. Her life class tutor, Paul, was heading for her corner.

"Haven't seen you for ages. You look exhausted. Are you still feeling unsettled after your travels?" he boomed.

The model's furry eyebrows bristled in all directions as if to distract her.

"I wish it were that simple," Moira said.

"It's four months since your trip to Europe."

"Yes, I know. This time West Sussex got to me, as well as the art course."

"Did you spend much time in London?"

"Enough to attend several theatre performances."

The smell of percolating coffee drifted over towards her. The Julian Ashton School of Painting held quality art courses, and offered quality coffee and tea. Moira had to admit that these days, art was what made her heart sing. It had fuelled her desire to visit the galleries in Europe and they had overwhelmed her with their treasures. In London she had spent hours in the National Gallery. London, Paris, Amsterdam, Vienna and Rome... her memories rocked about like a boat struggling against the constant movement of the sea. When would she be returning?

"It's good to see you still passionate about your art," said Graham.

Moira nodded in reply and recalled the days when her parents had disapproved of her going to art college. Instead they nudged her towards an arts degree and teaching, a proper career, as her mother put it. Alongside her demanding job in Sydney, Moira had completed a few art courses in the last four years, even sold a few paintings. On one occasion the buyer paid her more than the asking price, as she said it was too cheap.

"I know you've injected some life into your job by getting involved in school timetabling, or editing the school magazine, but you've been teaching English for so long you probably need a change," Paul said. "Anyway, try a pose from a different angle. A thirty-minute pose."

Moira moved her easel to another part of the studio. Drawing nudes helped her appreciate structure in forms. Once the broad strokes were completed, she was able to create contrast by applying shading. Life drawing helped her appreciate form. She found the male nude figure, with its angularity, much more challenging than the female.

The first hour passed quickly as Moira managed to concentrate. Then she excused herself and left early. The pain from her recent betrayal would still come and haunt her at times. She took a deep breath and made the effort to observe her surroundings. The lukewarm April sun heralded the approaching cooler weather of winter and illuminated The Argyle Centre in this area of The Rocks, which had been the seat of the first European settlement in Australia in 1788 and replaced the aboriginal settlement before it.

It had included, among other facilities, the administration centre, a hospital and a bakery. And, of course, the first convicts. Five minutes' walk and she was at Circular Quay, from where green ferries left heading for Mossman and Manly on the North Shore. Rested faces, reflecting the leisurely pace of a Saturday, replaced the strained and distressed expressions of the working week. The freshness of the scene gave her clarity of vision where she saw herself on a plateau of teaching achievements with no fresh goal ahead.

On returning to Randwick, she circled the area where she taught, as if the school buildings would give her answers. Thoughts came and went like the occasional clouds in the sky. She alternated between the desire to leave Guido and her fear of a financially uncertain future that a new life in England would entail. Indecision about what action to take led her to driving past her home. Gasping in disbelief, she turned the car around. Yes, there was a large FOR SALE sign, right outside their apartment.

Moira was outraged by Guido's action. How could he take a unilateral decision without consulting her? She had only been gone ten days. Moira phoned Martin, her neighbour. He had been a loyal friend.

"What's happening to our apartment? I saw the FOR SALE sign," she said, after they had exchanged greetings, hoping she didn't appear to be too concerned.

"I understand that Guido has a buyer for the apartment. It happened quite by chance apparently. Someone connected with his cycling activities. It's all going through," he said.

"I can't believe he has done this without talking to me about it," she said.

This turn of events pushed Moira over the edge with her decision making. It was time to leave Guido. She was no longer drowning in uncertainty. She cringed at her boldness. A fresh beginning is what she wanted. And she needn't necessarily stay in Australia. But did she have the courage to act?

If she returned to West Gidding, London's cultural events and art exhibitions would be one hour and fifteen minutes away by train and she wouldn't face the expenses that living in London entailed. A short journey from West Gidding to Newhaven accessed ferry crossings to France and would take her to the rest of Europe. Moira felt charged with new energy. Liz welcomed her at her house with an informal Chinese take away.

Liz Curtis had joined the English Department at the school where Moira taught, eighteen months ago after returning from a year-long working holiday in Europe. She had spent several months in London waitressing and teaching English to foreign students, then worked as a housemaid in a hotel in the Swiss Alps. Her enthusiasm for life was reflected in many stories about her experiences, which brought laughter to the normally sedate staff room. She had a habit of accompanying her tales by running her fingers through her tinted hair and giggling to herself.

Liz had always felt comfortable asking for teaching advice from the senior staff, and they were generous with their help. She felt in awe of Moira's achievements, whether they be rising to the challenge of demanding inspections for promotion, giving demonstration lessons for student teachers, or attending the meetings of the committee in charge of the NSW English syllabus. She had also worked with Moira on a project for migrant integration.

Liz had attended staffroom dinner outings to restaurants at the end of term so she knew Moira's two closest friends, and was one of the few invited to Moira's apartment for lunch during the school holidays – but had never met Guido. Liz supported Moira's latest passion for art as she herself had studied graphic design.

During the weekend, Moira spent a lot of time discussing her situation with Liz whose opinions she respected. Liz found it incomprehensible that Moira, who was intelligent and artistic, an accomplished teacher and administrator, couldn't make the leap to leading her life doing what she wanted – which was to live in England to develop her art work. Although Moira said she had made the decision to leave Guido and Sydney, her mind looked for excuses to rationalise staying in Sydney. Liz realised uprooting was, of course, a huge decision for Moira.

"Make a decision with your heart. Do you want to return to the UK? Yes or No? Then use your brain to solve the resulting problems. You have a beaut opportunity but only you can decide what action to take."

"Yes but..."

"No buts. You know you're not the first person to have left a marriage. Don't focus on issues that stop you from making the decision."

"OK."

"You can live your life to please others and never be totally alive, or you can please yourself."

"I suppose even Christopher Columbus must have had doubts and fears about his goal of discovering America. It was probably a case of *feel the fear but still do whatever you need to do*. You're not going to believe this, but as I was the eldest, I had to put my siblings' needs before my own. So it's a habit."

"A bad habit. You're an adult now so you create your own rules. You'll need a solicitor of course. Have you got one?"

"I haven't used a solicitor since we bought the apartment ten years ago."

"You could use my brother, James, if you like. I can ring him tonight," Liz said. "You can always return to Australia if it doesn't all work out for you, and in the meantime you will have had a great experience."

Moira clutched at the idea that she needed to speak to a solicitor before unravelling her Sydney life. Once again she was torn between the desire for a new life in England and her reluctance to abandon her financially comfortable life in Sydney.

Chapter 3

On Monday, James Curtis answered her questions about divorce when she consulted him.

"With regard to divorce, you automatically get it after a year's separation, under current legislation," he said. "If you return to England, the signed paperwork will go through and I will notify you when the decree comes through. Do you want to begin the process?"

"Yes," she said in a low voice after a moment's hesitation.

"Are you sure? Maybe you'd like some more time to think about it?"

She had unconsciously moved into decision-making mode since arriving at James' office. She signed all the required documents to activate the process. The process was seamless.

"Now with regards to your apartment, I presume you took out a mortgage in both names according to standard practice. How many more years before you pay it off?"

"I made the last payment a month ago and collected the title deeds from the building society."

"Where are the deeds?"

"I have them at my bank," she said.

"Collect them and bring them to me. I will need them for the sale of your apartment. Don't worry. Guido can't sell without the deeds if you leave them in my possession."

"One thing that matters to me is secrecy," Moira said.

James looked up from the documents and gazed at Moira.

"I don't want Guido knowing my whereabouts under any circumstances. I'll leave my contact address with you until I have a permanent address West Sussex."

"All the more reason to give me power of attorney."

"Yes of course. I am prepared to give up my share of the furniture, my books and my car as the price of my freedom. I have no desire to fight over every crystal glass or silver spoon."

After discussing the finer legal aspects of her situation with James and signing more documents, Moira returned to Liz's house.

She made out a list of *things to do*. Her first priority was to enter her apartment and collect her clothes, art materials, books, and most importantly of all, documents. Liz promised to go with Moira to support her. Moira remembered that Guido was going away on a business trip that week but his plans might have changed. She persuaded Liz to check up on this fact anonymously by ringing his secretary.

She felt like a thief, entering her own home. Her sadness was giving up the home that she had lovingly created herself. The sense of regret was tinged with the resolve to leave for ever. She left a brief note. Just a bald statement of fact.

I'm leaving you.

No reasons given. No arguments invited.

Liz remained sensitive to her mood changes. *It'll all work out* was soothing to Moira's ears especially when she had moments of doubt and uncertainty. They worked as a team, removing the items on her list from the apartment and loading up Liz's car. The rhythm of packing released the last of her attachment to her home. As it was a week day, few inhabitants of the building saw them. No one disturbed them.

When she returned to Liz's house, Moira felt weak. She hadn't eaten breakfast but accepting her break with the past was draining her emotions. Liz percolated some coffee which Moira gulped down. It was time to ring several shipping companies for quotations. Finally she chose a company that had contacts in the UK and a middle-of-the-range quotation. Liz helped to pack the three tea chests Moira had acquired in readiness for shipping to the UK. The company would pick them up the next day.

Equally emotional for Moira was her return to Head Office to offer her resignation form. The demanding climb up the executive ladder over ten years was erased with just one signature. All those hours, days, weeks and years of her devotion, ambitions, innovations, reduced to a signature. How humbling was that?

That evening, Liz opened a bottle of wine. As they sipped the celebratory drink, Liz suggested having a farewell dinner at a Greek restaurant where they could do line dancing. At the same time she started making a list of Moira's friends. Moira was tempted to accept the idea but instinct held her back.

"Liz, I would love a big group but people like to gossip. I still have to book my flight and want no accidental confrontation with Guido before I leave. I just can't risk meeting him."

"Surely you want to say goodbye to all your friends?"

"Yes, I wish I could. But it'll have to be a small group of us. People that Guido doesn't know. I'm sure I will be back in Australia for some reason or other in the future."

Liz registered Moira's flushed face and could see Moira wobbling in her resolve. She began to plan for an intimate group of five, while Moira spent the week closing bank accounts, terminating credit card agreements and ending her membership of the

National Gallery.

Fearful dreams filled Moira's sleep as she agonised all week how to tell her parents. Both were frail. Her mother had angina problems and her father had blocked arteries that were inoperable. She couldn't now visit them and dump her marital problems on them. The news might catapult them into shock. She also felt too vulnerable to handle any fallout from her latest revelations to her parents. Her consolation was that she had a week to consider the matter.

The one source of joy was buying a ticket to the UK. She had always fancied travelling with Singapore Airlines. The airline had a wonderful reputation for their Asian cuisine, food which she enjoyed. The travel agent pointed out that the return ticket was only a little more expensive then the single one. Might she not want to return to Australia? She considered this – it would leave her the opportunity to visit her parents at a later date. Yes, she would buy a return ticket. In some small measure, this appeased her sense of guilt about not seeing them before her departure from Sydney.

On Friday, her last evening in Sydney, Moira went out to dinner with Liz and three other friends. The venue was Doyle's Fish restaurant at Watson's Bay at the southerly side of the two Heads at the entrance to Sydney Harbour. It had been opened in 1885 and had operated under the stewardship of five generations of family. From their table they could see the Sydney Harbour Bridge with all the harbour life in front. The setting sun, with its last summer warmth, was shrouded in dramatic oranges and pinks. The sea lapped up to the water's edge. Sydney's oldest seafood restaurant was a fitting venue for her farewell meal. Moira inhaled the flavours of the juicy prawns. They chose John Dory, one of the most tender of local fish. Crisp Chablis accompanied the seafood.

It felt like a secret society gathering, where they were celebrating a social occasion while the rest of the world followed its usual routines, unaware of Moira's momentous decision. Though it still felt daunting to her, she felt her supportive friends were being swept along with the excitement, as if they too wished to drop everything and start a new life. For Moira it was also an opportunity to relax after a hectic and emotionally taxing week. She left them Scarlett's address.

That evening Moira set about writing a letter to her parents. Perhaps the wine had mellowed her concern for their welfare. It was wiser to inform her parents that she had left Guido, though she didn't think he would have the gall to contact them. Her hand shook slightly. Writing to her parents was as nerve-racking as leaving Guido or her job, but felt more appropriate than stumbling over words on the phone.

Dear Ma and Pa

By the time you receive this letter, I'll have landed in England.

You may well ask whether I am attending another art course!? I hope to ...but more significantly...I've left Guido for good. He doesn't know where I am or what I intend to do. I left him a brief note to say I was leaving him. He may well try to get my address from you. Please don't let him have it.

I'm fine now that I've actually made the decision to leave him.

I've left power of attorney with my lawyer and he has started divorce proceedings on my behalf. He will also attend to the sale of the apartment.

I'm enclosing my temporary address: c/o-Scarlett Hughes, Primrose Cottage, Bramley, West Sussex, BN41 2HH, UK.

My ticket to the UK is a return ticket.

I'll write again when I arrive in England

Lots of love

Moira

The words sounded so clinical but the truth was best. She trusted that they knew her well enough to let her go her way. Moira stuck the stamp on the envelope. On the Saturday evening, she posted the letter just before flying out of Sydney.

Relieved, she was ready for her return to West Gidding, her pores oozing with optimism.

Guido was driving from Bathurst at a steady one hundred and ten kilometres an hour. At this rate he would be in Sydney in three hours' time. Just as well he had drunk three cups of coffee at breakfast, he needed to stay awake. His sales had been promising that week. The landscape he was passing was parched and bleached by the previous summer and still the heat enveloped him, despite the air conditioning in his company car. He would welcome the breezes that came off the sea at home – and the G&T on the terrace as well. He hoped he and Moira could patch things up when she returned, and life would return to the usual routine. And maybe there would be news about the sale of the apartment.

Guido was looking forward to returning to sophisticated eating in Sydney restaurants, home comforts and joining some of his mates who cycled around Centennial Park. The daily exercise kept him fit. The fact that he had been away didn't matter, as it was only a small group and they couldn't cycle in the park more than two abreast.

As soon as Guido entered the apartment, he

headed for the bedroom. A shower would be refreshing after the long drive. As he opened the sliding doors to the wardrobe, the vacuum in Moira's part of the wardrobe became very obvious. Apart from a handful of clothes, everything had gone. He began to feel uneasy. Guido touched the $100 red suede high heels he had bought her for her last birthday almost with tenderness. Maybe her departure wasn't permanent. He sprinted through to the room she used as a studio. Many of the brushes and oil paint tubes had been removed. His shoulders tensed up. He poked his head through the door in the lounge. The painting by Pro Hart that her parents had given her was missing. The rectangle of differently coloured paint on the wall was all that remained of the painting.

Finally he reached the kitchen. There was a note on the table.

I'm leaving you.

No greeting. No explanations. No signature. The words seemed unreal. He felt spaced out and faint. He still loved her. How could she do this to him?

Then these feelings were replaced by sharp anger. How dare she walk out on him? Rattled, Guido left the empty shell of a home to drown his sorrows.

After the long journey from Sydney, the Singapore Airlines 707 was circling around Heathrow International Airport. Moira had hardly slept on the journey. Her mouth felt dry, her sinuses were beginning to ache from the air conditioning, she was tired of the metallic taste of food, and her feet were swollen. She'd indulged in a couple of glasses of wine at the beginning of the trip. Too late to do anything about that now.

Moira wondered how she would find West Sussex this time. Since her return to Australia in January, she had been following the UK news regularly. She had read with interest about the changes Margaret Thatcher had brought in. Her confrontation with the striking miners only ended last March. So life for the Brits in 1985 was looking up. Everyone expected to have at least one holiday a year abroad.

"Place your seats in the upright position and fasten your seat belts."

Moira tuned into what the air hostess was saying, stacked the plastic cups and made an attempt to tidy up her viewing post for landing. Some of the passengers around her started to sort out their hand luggage.

The captain announced that the temperature on this spring Monday was fourteen degrees centigrade and the local time was 8 am. At least it wasn't raining. Moira adjusted her watch. The flight was late. She hoped Scarlett would be at the airport to meet her. She hadn't heard from her in the last few days.

Clutching her heavy hand luggage stuffed with precious documents and a change of clothing, Moira held on to the rail as she staggered down the steps to the airport bus. Now for Immigration. She knew her Australian passport would be automatically stamped with a six month visa.

Of course, the UK was not new for her. She had lived there with her family until the age of ten. She had spent a working holiday in the UK when she left university. Then recently, she had spent two months in the UK during the Australian summer school holidays. The massive queues snaked their way through to passport control. The arrivals moved forward slowly. Several flights had arrived simultaneously. A baby started to grizzle, venting its frustration in ever louder screaming.

"Moira Capaldi?"

"Yes, that's me,"

"What's the reason for your arrival in the UK?" the female immigration officer said. She straightened herself up and bristled with officialdom.

"I'm here in the UK to start a new life..." Moira replied happy to launch into all the details of her future plans.

"Do you have a residency visa?" the officer interrupted without looking up.

"No, but I used to have a British passport..."

"But you don't have one now?"

"It expired. I have to go to the Home Office to get a new one."

The officer was stamping her Australian passport and waved her through the gate. Moira checked the stamped page and was shocked to see a visa stamp for two months only. Her heart sank and her legs were unsteady. She should have kept her mouth shut. She had forgotten that with bureaucracy, the fewer words said the better. She hoped things would improve.

She collected her hold luggage from the carousel. Her large suitcase contained her precious possessions, a selection of her best clothes and some painting materials. She trudged through the long winding corridors of the terminal and finally into Customs. There she was faced with a motley group of waiting people. Plenty of buzz. Some held placards with names, but no Scarlett. She wasn't panicking but…

Chapter 4

It was then that Scarlett glided into the forecourt of the arrivals lounge. As usual her make-up was flawless, and her chic pants and top emphasised her willowy figure. The vibrant emerald green of the blouse contrasted with her shining jet black hair. In her early twenties she had been one of the English Bluebells who had danced at the Lido in Paris. The Bluebells were as well known in the UK as the Rockettes in New York.

Her upright posture reflected the dance training of the past and took years off her age. In contrast, Moira, hunched under the weight of the suitcase, felt as crushed as the blouse she was wearing. She forced a smile on to her face, dumped her luggage and ran forward to greet her friend.

"So pleased you came." They hugged.

"Despite the jet lag, you look well."

"So how is school?"

Scarlett was now teaching in a school not far from West Gidding.

"We're on holiday. At the end of term I was so knackered."

Moira had been so absorbed by her own plans she had forgotten about the English school term schedules. Scarlett picked up Moira's hand luggage and they both wended their way out of the terminal. They strained to hear each other above the echoing background noise as each gave a quick synopsis of recent events. They were glad to leave the jungle of people in the airport. Scarlett commented on how difficult it had been to park her car. Outside the sky was swollen with grey clouds creating an impression of gloom. When they reached the car park, Moira was amazed to see her friend opening the boot of a red Jensen Healey sports car.

"How long have you had this gem?"

"Just bought it recently. The therapist said I had to pamper myself," Scarlett said with a smug smile on her face.

She had told Moira she was having difficulties in her marriage when they met at the art weekend workshop last January. The numbers in the workshop had been low and so they had been able to chat while painting in the studio. Scarlett had an effervescent personality and laughed a lot.

"Impressive."

They set off for West Gidding. Moira felt relieved to be in the comfort of Scarlett's car instead of travelling by public transport. They negotiated the heavy traffic around Heathrow and found themselves on a stretch of congested motorway. An eerie haze of mist shrouded the side roads; tall trees speared through, adding to the spooky atmosphere. At least now they were able to converse more easily.

"No regrets about your decision?" said Scarlett giving Moira a searching look sideways.

"No. It's just that the Passport Control Officer has created problems for me. Otherwise I'm fine."

"Then let's go out for dinner tonight. You'll have plenty of time to have a nap, a shower and change your clothes."

"You're an angel. Thanks so much for picking me up at Heathrow. By the way how is your painting getting on?"

“It’s not. I’m needing to focus on what to do about my marriage. Nick is a good man, but we have nothing in common these days. I don’t know what to do.”

“I see.”

Moira nodded as if understanding the dilemma. What a coincidence that both of them were experiencing problems in their marriage.

The trip took over an hour, and brought back the memories of her week-long stay last January. West Gidding was built on flat land during the Middle Ages. With fewer than five thousand people, it stretched beyond the South Downs, so beloved by walkers.

She had forgotten how the fifteenth century flint cottages with handkerchief sized gardens formed an irregular line down the length of Main Street. Scarlett pulled up at a B&B, a one storey building graced by an established garden, situated on the opposite side where the houses were of the red brick so popular in West Sussex. Moira asked if there were any vacancies. There were none. Not good. The owner suggested calling at the other B&B on the outskirts of the village, a five minute drive away. Otherwise there were the three local pubs. Bleary-eyed, she hoped they would have better luck there.

The second B&B was a large modern pebble dash bungalow, not Moira's style at all. But she needed a roof over her head. A room with its own entrance was available for the rest of the week, so she booked it for four nights. Scarlett took the phone details and said she would return at 6:30 pm. Moira dumped her case and bag on the floor of her room. It looked out on to the front garden and contained twin beds, a table and an armchair. The mirrored, sliding doors of the wardrobe helped to create the illusion of space. To Moira, the room seemed to be without character: clinical.

After the deafening traffic around Heathrow Airport, West Gidding was quiet. Only occasional traffic sounds and silence. Moira lay on her bed for a moment, luxuriating in its balance between comfort and firmness. Her eyes felt gritty with lack of sleep;

she closed them and her brain felt as if it was melting. Soon she was breathing deeply.

When Moira woke up the curtains were still open and she checked her watch; it was 10 am early Tuesday morning. She had slept through a day and a night. She would need to ring Scarlett about missing dinner. Clambering out of bed, she allowed the lukewarm sunshine to hug her nakedness as she readied herself for a shower. After digging out some crushed clothes from her suitcase, she went downstairs. Breakfast time was coming to an end. Her stomach was rumbling, and thankfully the cook agreed to make her an English breakfast of eggs and sausages, tomatoes and mushrooms. The stark reality challenging her was that she was homeless, without work and with limited finances. Her former life had unravelled.

After eating her comfort food, Moira strolled towards the centre of the village. The modern buildings around her B&B were lacking in character; they looked like council houses. It wasn't raining and the sun was a bleached yellow.

She recalled from her last visit that West Gidding had an array of shops with essential items for sale in Main Street. She could browse through those this morning. When settled into more permanent accommodation, she would have to find a way of getting to Worthing for her weekly shopping at Sainsbury's, the local supermarket. West Gidding didn't have a chocolate box look, but as a village it was not part of a fully-fledged consumer society either.

As Moira strolled up the cobbled streets, so different to the tarmac roads she was used to in Sydney, not that she walked much there, she found that strangers were friendly enough to say *Hello,* which she hadn't expected. *Small villages didn't like strangers,* she had been told. Ladies were armed with their traditional wicker shopping baskets. She found the upmarket deli tempting; the French patés and nests of cheeses peeped out of the display counter. She bought some Red Leicester cheese, and ham, with salad and rather expensive fruit from the greengrocer. Her shopping was completed with a purchase of freshly baked rolls from the family bakery. Their smell had enticed her, though she suspected the roll would have the texture of cotton wool. Bread lacked any substance these days as producers cut back on wholesome ingredients. She noticed a laundrette at the other end of the row of shops; she would drop off her soiled clothes later.

Satisfied with her food purchases, she called at the Post Office. It didn't only sell stamps; she was surprised to see newspapers, confectionery, ice cream, frozen and tinned foods, as well as household items on offer. She resolved to return to buy more items once she found a place to rent. A large notice board with an array of local advertisements caught her eye; the loose cards flapped every time the door opened. She asked for a card and scrawled out her *Looking for a Room to Rent* message, then pinned it on to the board.

She crossed the narrow street and noticed a red telephone box. After struggling to identify the coins, she took out the ten pence coin and pushed it in the slot. Would Scarlett be in? After the third ring, there was a reply.

"Hello, it's me." she said. The response was an outburst of giggles.

"Has Sleeping Beauty woken up yet?" Scarlett asked. More chuckles followed. "I know you were very tired when I picked you up from the airport yesterday. I left a message for you. Did you get it?" Without waiting for an answer, "Ready for a night out this evening?"

"Sure."

"We'll catch up properly. I'll pick you up at 6:30 pm. See you then. Have to rush now. Bye."

So people in this small village rushed? How strange. She would take her time. She sauntered down Main Street away from the shops and noticed a sign saying *West Gidding Gallery*. It was a flint cottage, one of a row, matching the others in size. As she entered, the doorbell tinkled. On the inside, the walls of the fifteenth century cottage were painted white, a fitting background to the landscapes and still lifes in water colours. The current exhibition was spread over three rooms. The leaded windows set into the deep walls let in little natural light, so spotlights had been fitted into the ceiling to illuminate the paintings.

Information sheets, with the titles of the paintings and prices, lay on a small table. Asian rugs were scattered over the plain wooden floors and a jug of tulips decorated the desk, where a dark-haired lady sat doing some office work. She was dressed in well-cut, arty clothes, chunks of amber hugging her thin neck.

"Welcome to West Gidding Gallery," she said formally.

Moira noticed how her high cheek bones were emphasized by the severe haircut which resembled an upside down bowl, with no layers to soften the severity.

"You came at the right time. Today is a quiet morning."

She returned to the work on her desk. Moira browsed around. The traditional water colours were skilfully painted. She picked up a well-designed brochure, and discovered that the exhibiting artist was

Felicity Green. Once Moira had finished her rounds, the lady introduced herself as Zara James.

"I'm Moira Capaldi."

"You are visiting West Gidding, yes?" she said.

"I attended an art course in West Gidding last January and met up with Scarlett Hughes. Now I have returned hoping to stay here."

"I know her. West Gidding is a small place and we all know each other."

"I enjoyed being in England. The trip gave me a fresh perspective on life. When I returned to Australia, I had a rethink about my priorities in life and decided to return here."

"A big change, no?"

As Moira was leaving she whirled around and asked if there was any chance of working in the gallery. Zara's eyebrows shot upwards but she composed herself with a brief reply,

"No, I'm afraid. Excuse me please. I need to attend to something at the back."

Was that an excuse to disappear Moira wondered?

At that moment, the doorbell rang and a tall man entered the gallery. Dark haired and clean shaven, he looked distinguished in a well cut suit. His sense of presence was palpable. He held out his hand and introduced himself,

"I'm Michael Upton. I dropped in on the off-chance Zara was here."

His eyes lasered into hers. For a moment he seemed to be looking into her very soul with his intense blue eyes.

"I'm Moira Capaldi."

She had difficulty in maintaining eye contact with him. His smile, crooked at one end of his mouth, was hesitant, as if taking in her features, studying her. He was still holding her hand.

"Call me Mike," his voice was soft and silky.

The energy entering her body through his hand was making her feel flustered. If she didn't remove her hand, the blush that had started at her neck would spread to her face. But who was he? Was he Zara's man? As if reading her thoughts, he announced, "I am Zara's lawyer."

She had to deliberately disentangle her hand from his. She was thirty-eight years old, a mature woman, yet she was acting like a twenty year old. Just then Zara came back to her desk.

"Good morning Mike. Sorry I couldn't come to see you yesterday. Something urgent came up."

She headed for her filing cabinet.

"If you still want to see me, come to the office at noon."

"Fine. Will do."

Moira eased her way out through the front door.

"Enjoy West Gidding, Moira," called out Zara.

Moira was still flustered by her meeting with Michael. Some fresh air would cool her down. She sauntered up to the deli to buy some lunch. On the way out of the shop, she was so preoccupied with her thoughts that she strode into the person coming out of a doorway on her left. The impact made her drop her bags of food.

"Sorry," she said automatically and her first impulse was to look for the scattered bags. Only then did she look the man in the eye. It was Michael Upton.

He was apologetic as he bent down to the ground, to her eye level, and picked up the bags with her.

"We are destined to meet," he said. Moira flushed. "Perhaps I can make it up to you. Will you come out to lunch with me?"

Moira registered surprise. Her lips remained closed.

"What about the weekend?" Mike continued.

She nodded.

"I'll pick you up at 10 am, Sunday," he said.

"Fine. Thank you," she replied. Her brain felt like putty.

"Can I have your phone number?"

"I don't actually have one yet?"

"Well, how about I pick you up from the front door of the gallery?"

Finally she cleared her throat and found her voice.

"That's kind of you."

He waved goodbye and strode out in the opposite direction. In this small village everyone with their insatiable curiosity would have them labelled as a couple after the first outing. She would have to make sure they went out somewhere well away from West Gidding. She looked at her lunch. It was unappetising in its shattered state; she tossed it into a rubbish bin. Diet time.

Moira returned to her stark B&B room. Her priority was to visit the Home Office in London to extend her visa. She recalled how she had been grounded from flying as an air hostess for Qantas after her training finished, until such time as her Australian passport was processed. After all that she had forgotten to renew her British passport. She hoped she would be over her jet lag by Thursday as she would aim to be the first in the queue and that meant leaving West Gidding by bus around 6 am. Her second priority was to find a place to live in.

Chapter 5

Mike had never experienced emotional fireworks as a result of a handshake. He couldn't believe he had hung on so long to Moira's hand; it was as if it had magnetised him. So when Moira lurched into him at the deli, he felt he had to seize the moment to engage socially with her. He wondered whether the dryness of his legal work had kept his feeling nature shuttered away. His compartmentalised world was crashing about him. He was used to being in control of his social life as well as his legal work.

Moira's jeans and sweater were ordinary enough. It was the way she moved her body that made those clothes hang on her like designer items; sophistication exuded from her. If Moira was to stand beside Margaret, whom he had met through a dating agency a few weeks before, Margaret would be eclipsed. Just as well he had told Margaret the first time he took her to dinner that he was only interested in companionship. Last time they met, Margaret was suggesting they should think about moving into together. That woke him up and he had to be blunt. No moving in and no babies.

Although the encounter in the art gallery was the first time he had met Moira, he had picked up on the strong chemistry between them. Moira fascinated him; he needed to find out more about her.

What a romantic fool he was. He still knew so little about her. She might be married. If she had relationship ties in Australia, she might well drift back there. Well, he would have to wait and see.

Nonetheless, nothing was going to stop him from spending time with Moira and becoming friends, and if it was his destiny, more than friends.

Scarlett arrived on time. Looking forward to the evening, Moira slid into the passenger seat. It was a balmy evening, rare during an English spring. Daylight would last until about 9 pm, something she appreciated in England. Scarlett had selected a bistro in a neighbouring village where they could have anything from a soup to a three course meal. Moira realised that Scarlett was watching her weight. From past experience she was aware she herself could easily put on half a stone or more, as a colder climate always made her more hungry.

The waiter led them through the restaurant to their reserved table. It was in a discreet alcove away from the main eating area, so they wouldn't have to talk over the voices of strangers at the next table. He flicked out the cream linen napkin and placed it on Moira's lap. Scarlett shook out her own. They ordered Chablis, and oysters for starters. Moira chose a traditional roast lamb – something substantial after the tasteless flight fodder and missed meals yesterday. Scarlett opted for a beef salad. Moira's intense curiosity simmered beneath the mask of serenity; finally she could wait no longer and said, "So, tell me about Nick and you."

"Since I saw you last I have been going to therapy."

"That's a big step to take."

"Well, I was really getting dissatisfied with my marriage to Nick. He is a lot older than me. In the sessions I came to understand that I had chosen to fall in love with a father figure, to feel safe in the relationship. Of course I didn't realise all this when I met him." She played with her napkin. "The age difference was not an issue early in the marriage. However now that I am in my early forties and Nick is in his late fifties, our lives follow different paths. He likes to stay at home, watch television, and go to sleep early. I like to go to my art classes, I enjoy a social life, with or without him, and our sex life has virtually ground to a halt. He doesn't want to go and speak to a doctor about his health or his sex drive, so I'm reassessing my marriage."

"And have you come to any decisions yet?"

"I'm pulled two ways. I'm dissatisfied with our present set up but at the same time I keep reminding myself that I shouldn't forget the good times we had together – when we went on holidays in the UK or travelled to Europe. He also supported me financially while I was studying."

"Just as well you don't have children."

"Yes. So I'm continuing with therapy. Let's see what happens." Love was such a slippery thing.

Moira gulped. Scarlett's description made Moira's hairs stand on end. It felt as if Scarlett was mirroring her own life but in a different way. She hesitated. How much should she share?

"You can trust me. I won't repeat anything you say," said Scarlett, intuiting that Moira craved to share a confidence.

"Guido met me while I was working for Qantas. He was romantic. Though I lived through the flower power era and open sex revolution, I didn't choose to live like that. I had a childhood sweetheart for many years and that broke up when I joined Qantas. Guido and I married without living together, no doubt the remnants of my religious upbringing." Moira took a deep breath and frowned as if dredging up memories. "Marriage is like champagne. It can lose its fizz."

Scarlett laughed, "Too true."

Moira's thoughts tumbled over one another.

"He wined and dined me, but that all changed when his business ventures failed." She took another forkful of food. "Luckily I had taken a secure teaching position with the state education department, so bills were paid on time. I had known he liked his drink during our courting days, but now his drinking intensified. Maybe business problems which he didn't like to discuss with me." She ran her fingers through her hair. "At the same time, he started to flirt with women at parties in front of me. If I made comments about this at home, his face would go red with anger, his voice grew louder, and then he would walk out of the apartment." She rolled her eyes. "He probably joined his sporting buddies at the pub as he would return home reeking of alcohol. I felt his reactions were always disproportionate to the situation, but it could have been his second-generation Italian temperament emerging. Who knows? It was easier to excuse Guido's angry outbursts in the early days of our marriage when he made an effort to please me".

Moira tailed off, sipping her wine; her recollections bringing up feelings that were uncomfortable.

"After the first flush of sex, we were left with little in common. He always claimed he didn't want children. Guido wasn't interested in my theatre outings and health farm visits; I didn't enjoy the social life with excessive drinking that people in sport enjoy."

"So you led separate lives?"

"Yes. I went to Europe on my own twice. He had no desire to share any of that. He preferred to visit friends in Australia."

"Did you talk about this to your parents?"

"There was no point. They only saw us when we visited. I sometimes went on my own. They would not have approved of me leaving him, for religious reasons."

They tackled their main course. Moira's roast lamb was served with mint jelly; the roast vegetables served on a separate plate looked appetising. They ate in amicable silence for a few minutes.

"So what led you to resigning from your job and coming back here this time?" Scarlett changed her questioning.

"There was drama. I'm not ready to discuss it. Things happened. The upshot was that Guido put our apartment on the market while I was away and I decided to return to the UK to pursue my art rather than go through a break up in Sydney."

"I see what you mean about fate forcing your hand, Moira."

"Thanks for listening."

Scarlett instinctively felt that her friend's dramatic decision to leave Sydney was waking up emotions inside her. She felt there was more to the story, but didn't want to push Moira too hard.

"Be careful who you share this with. Gossip is rife in a village the size of West Gidding." Yes, she would have to be watchful. Moira had been used to the gift of anonymity that Sydney offered her.

"I'm glad I enjoyed my recent holiday in England. I still had the money to splash around. Now it seems I have my freedom but little money."

"Things have a way of working out. You'll see." Scarlett just laughed.

They had enjoyed their meal but perhaps the serious turn of conversation had challenged them both. They asked for the bill to be brought and Scarlett started looking for her car keys.

Moira opened the car door.

"How about we go walking together, get out and explore the Downs?"

When Moira pulled a face, and looked at the clouds forming above them, Scarlett chuckled.

"Moira, you're going to have to get used to the rain or you'll miss out on life and the outdoors in England. Just get yourself a waxed Barbour jacket and you will be fine. How about Wednesday week?"

Moira agreed.

"See you then."

And they parted. Scarlett was right. She had to make an effort to adapt to the climate. Now she understood why the British talked so much about the weather; outdoor activities could be scuppered so easily. Aloneness took her to bed early that night.

Thousands of miles from her home, her work, her friends, and her professional reputation, Moira felt stripped of her self-esteem and confidence. It took time to create a reputation at work. Her decision to walk out of her life in Sydney had been impulsive and a huge risk. She had to admit that she was missing her former lifestyle, though the thought of Guido's betrayal and attempted apartment sale felt like a knife plunging into her heart. The wound was ever-present, despite the changes in her life. She pushed the disturbing thoughts aside, shaped her duvet into a cocoon and snuggled inside.

On Wednesday, Moira woke up to a wedge of sunlight between the curtains. She was still jet-lagged, and tired after her dinner with Scarlett. She would lie in this morning. Her thoughts about her forthcoming London visit fluttered through her mind like butterflies. Moira was thrilled about returning to London.

She had often come to London as an air hostess with the Australian airlines: in those pre-jumbo days, long haul trips all ended in London. Her routes had been Singapore, Bahrain and London or Hong Kong, Teheran, London with occasional stops at Manila, Athens or Frankfurt. All that now seemed part of the hazy past, but she was filled with nostalgia for the carefree lifestyle for her mid-twenties.

In the late sixties, London had been the cultural hub of Europe. Like the rest of Great Britain, it had struggled through the post war years in the 1950s. The 1960s brought the Beatles with their catchy, exciting music, and the younger generation had rebelled against conservative values, in those marihuana-filled days. Qantas crews were fortunate enough to stay at the Mayfair Hotel, so theatre visits were what Moira liked to organise on arrival. Window shopping didn't cost anything and she could enjoy the elegance of the shops in New Bond Street. Nameless and anonymous, she often strolled through Mayfair and Knightsbridge. Green Park was one of her favourite spaces in the city, with lots of mature trees, including magnolias which dropped their waxy petals on the grass.

Later as she sauntered along Main Street, a large signpost further down caught her eye: *West Gidding School of English.* It was attached to a Victorian building with two storeys above ground level. The need to find a source of income uppermost in her mind, she entered the building and asked the receptionist whether she could speak to the Director of the School.

"I'm sorry but Tony Carter went on a day excursion to Brighton Pavilion with the students. Could you come back tomorrow?"

"I'm off to London tomorrow. Perhaps I will call on Friday."

Moira didn't want to tie herself into an appointment time yet. She was still hoping that there might be a response to her *Looking for Room to Rent* card at the Post Office, and she needed to be flexible. It was all very well to close down her Sydney life in five days but it would take much longer to set up her West Sussex life.

Moira returned to the Post Office to purchase her bus ticket to Shoreham station and pick up a train timetable. On impulse she bought a Cadbury's chocolate bar to accompany her on the train journey to London, reflecting that her craving for chocolate was always fuelled by anxiety. Moira returned to the B&B, postponing a decision about extending her stay there until Friday. Sleep was slow in coming that night because of her excitement at returning to London; she wondered whether it had changed much.

Chapter 6

Next day Moira arrived at Shoreham Station by an early bus and checked the platform number. The train journey would take an hour and fifteen minutes. She had brought her little pocket book of London street maps, but was never one to spend much time reading on trains as she found it difficult to keep her eyes on the text while the train sashayed along. She turned her attention to the people about her: regular commuters were preoccupied with reading their newspapers, some were enjoying an extra nap. The skies were heavy with grey clouds, but they were not going to dampen her enthusiasm for visiting London.

She would need to change trains at Victoria Station in order to reach West Croydon, and from there she would be able to walk to the home of the Home Office. Strange that the office was so far from central London. Her stomach churned over at the thought of dealing with bureaucracy.

At Victoria Station, the commuters speeded towards the ticket collection points and then flocked through the exits. She took the time to find her bearings; she wasn't used to public transport. On the train to West Croydon, she recalled an incident from her air hostessing days: after spending her holidays in Europe, she was due back in London to work on a flight returning to Sydney. The stress of trying to get out of Communist Hungary, when all flights had been cancelled due to bad weather, was what led her to leave her handbag on the London Underground the following day. She had been lucky because it had been handed in to an office at the next Tube station. Under pressure, one could do strange things.

On arrival at West Croydon, she patted her passport in the inside pocket of her jacket and set off for the Home Office. She recognised the tall modern buildings that she had seen in a photo. Lunar House and Apollo House had been built in the 1970s. She couldn't help feeling that all these post-war buildings had no character. She disliked bureaucracy, but she had to put up with it, or return to Australia. So, irritating as it might be, she entered the building.

The reception was manned by an official who

originated from India and was occupied at a filing cabinet. He stumbled out of his chair and shuffled over to the front desk. Moira explained she wanted information about extending her visa for the UK. He directed her to another part of the same building. The processing would be trying. This time it was a bumptious British woman who obviously relished her position of power, and bullied worried arrivals.

"Yes?" she asked. The other officials had at least greeted her with a "Good morning."

"I'd like to speak to someone about visas for the UK".

"Walk along the corridor and turn right. That's where the office is for migrants."

Moira leaned over the desk, "I'm not a migrant. I used to live in the UK. Would you mind directing me to someone who could help me with extending my visa?"

"OK here's the number for your queue," she said. The woman smiled, and directed her to the waiting room. Fifteen people. Mostly from the Commonwealth. So she might have to wait for a while for them to be processed. This would give her time to prepare her strategy for presenting her facts. Remembering her experience at Immigration in the airport, Moira decided to avoid personal comments.

When her number was eventually called, Moira took a deep breath and marched into the interview room. A middle aged woman was sitting behind a desk covered with files and she introduced herself as Mary Reid. Moira explained that when she recently arrived in the UK, she had received a two month visa in her Australian passport, that she had lived in the UK until she was ten years old, had lost any previous records and wanted to extend her visas.

"There's no problem in applying for an extension of this visa but that will take time," Mary said. "If you currently have a two month visa, I suggest you start the process of establishing your permanent residency. To do that, you have to prove when you were living in the UK."

The woman was courteous and efficient. Moira listened. Mary continued with the list of documents required: her father's passport, expired or not, the letter of his appointment to a job in South Australia, or any papers confirming her schooling. Furthermore, all had to be originals and not copies. Mary also gave her the phone numbers for the Police Constabulary in Scotland and the National Insurance Office.

"The documents will be double checked and then a permanent residency stamp will be placed in your Australian passport. When does that passport expire?"

"In two years' time. Is that a problem?"

"Not if you apply for your British passport in the meantime. Do that as soon as you receive the permanent residency stamp. Hold on to all original documents for the passport application. Keep the reference number I am allocating and the phone number, including my extension number."

As Moira left Mary's office, she was aware of her shoulders dropping. With her head aching, her stomach rumbling, her limbs weak as if after heavy exercise, she chafed with frustration. She wanted to get back into central London, away from officialdom and red tape, as quickly as possible. Once on the train back to Victoria Station, she stretched her arms out to release the tension from her shoulders.

Central London felt humid but the air had warmed up. She slowed down the pace of her walking. The streets were cheered up by the presence of flower stalls; it was too early for summer flowers, but tulips and the last of the daffodils were on sale. As she drew closer to Oxford Street, she noticed a few café customers sitting at tables outside. A coffee while watching the world go by would suit her; a shopping trip to Marks & Spencer could wait. She had read that Mohammad Al Fayed had purchased Harrods, putting an end to a long English tradition. Perhaps this was the beginning of a new trend when foreigners would buy up chunks of London.

Though a cosmopolitan city, attracting tourists from all over the world for its pageantry and history, London still appeared uniquely English to Moira's Australian eyes. She observed that most people in the city centre wore smart clothes, although jeans were common in the streets, usually worn by luggage-conscious tourists. Men still liked to wear hats, and of course everyone carried the obligatory umbrella. She was still irritated by the regular showers so common in the springtime.

Moira was very aware that the 1980s were a time of innovation in the UK. It was a year of *firsts*. The first British mobile call had been made last January and the first House of Lords' debate had been televised. Elsewhere in the same months the FDA had developed a test for screening blood for AIDS, the first successful heart transplant had taken place, and Windows 1.0 had been released. Discoveries led to optimism. These events were paralleled by significant political change overseas. *Glasnost* was the new buzz word. Gorbachev had become the new leader of the Soviet Union, and in the United States, Ronald Reagan was sworn in for his second term of office.

She breathed in the not-so-fresh air in New Bond Street. When the waiter arrived she ordered a cappuccino. The sun warmed her back. The increased noise levels assaulted her: cars honked, brakes squealed. London was churned up. Her favourite city was now screaming out for attention, with a confused jumble of noises which were jagged rather than comforting.

London had always been known for its dining. In the late 1960s the restaurants had been mainly French, Italian, Chinese and Indian with exceptions such as *Daquise* in South Kensington which catered for post-war Polish exiles. The British taste-buds showed signs of change. Restaurants now offered food from every continent in the world. Pubs joined the international throng and were keen to offer foreign dishes at economical prices.

Moira bought the *Telegraph* to check out the programmes in the West End theatres. She skimmed through it, seeing that the prices were at least £20 or more for evening tickets, and no matinees were offering cheaper prices today. The sinking feeling that she could no longer afford such entertainment left her feeling dismayed. Theatre and concerts had been such an integral part of her life, but it looked as if these would be the first items to be dropped in her times of austerity measures. This would be the price she had to pay for her new freedom.

She meandered on to the National Gallery, where she viewed the Impressionists at her leisure. At least that was free. Moira enjoyed sitting down on the wooden benches and taking time to digest the paintings slowly. The paintings always looked different every time she viewed them, probably because she noticed new things about them every time she saw them. No book illustration ever fully did justice to the scale of a painting, or its colours.

Restored in spirit, she turned her attention to returning to West Gidding. On the way to the station she passed a Post Office. Scarlett had suggested she buy herself two phonecards, one domestic and one international as they were the most economical way of paying for phone calls, so she called in to purchase them.

As the train to Shoreham shuddered forward, she allowed herself to observe the countryside and admire its vivid greenness between short naps. Her visa problems had not been solved but at least she had a plan of action. Feeling low occurred when she was tired. She closed her eyes and started to doze. Her dreams were filled with writing letters, dealing with rejection from government officials and villains deciding her visa fate, not necessarily in that order.

When she arrived back at her B&B, her landlady told her that a Pat Myles had rung about an advertisement of hers and had left a phone number. Would Moira please return the call? Moira was eager to try out her phone card. A vibrant, friendly voice replied. Pat introduced herself and said she had seen Moira's notice in the Post Office. Was Moira still interested in renting a room?

"I am still looking, yes. What's your address?" asked Moira.

"36 Main Street."

Moira almost whooped with delight. Lady Luck was on her side: her favourite street. "May I come round to see the room?"

"Of course. Cooking facilities and bathroom are next door. When would you like to come?"

"Tomorrow at 10 am?"

"Fine. Look forward to meeting you."

Next day, after fortifying herself with breakfast, Moira made her way to the address she had been given. Walking along Main Street, she passed the art gallery. Zara was readjusting a painting in the window. On impulse Moira waved and Zara recognized her and waved back. She continued her walk to number 36.

Pat welcomed her as she entered the cottage. There was a musty smell about the entrance hall that did nothing to enhance the white-painted wattle and daub walls with their black beams. Pat led her up a narrow staircase. The squeaks on the staircase revealed it was wooden despite the softness underfoot where Berber carpet added warmth. They reached the top of the winding staircase where they came across three stained doors, fashioned out of panels of unpolished wood. The original metal latches were painted black. Moira hoped there was a more modern security measure on the other side of the doors.

Pat lifted the latch on the left to step into the bedroom, a large, spacious room that was also painted brilliant white. Moira was aware of an uneasy drop in temperature. The furnishings were simple but tasteful: a double bed, a bedside table, a wooden wardrobe, an oak antique writing desk, and a wingback chair which stood by the small windows which overlooked Main Street. The curtains were of fine silk in a vibrant emerald green. The room looked stylish but exuded homeliness and comfort. Pat must have cleaned the room for her inspection as it was spotless. Pat pointed out the modern central heating. Moira wondered where the cooking facilities and bathroom that Pat had spoken of might be.

As if reading her mind, Pat led Moira back out on the landing,

"There's more, you know," as she led her through the middle door into a shower room with basin, toilet and Yale lock on the inside. Moira found that post-war bathrooms in the UK were tricky. This one was large and had been modernised. At least she wouldn't be squashed sitting on the toilet seat. The third door closed off a kitchenette with a wooden cupboard for storing food, two electric rings for cooking, a small fridge and an electric jug. Basic, modern but adequate for producing simple meals if she could be bothered to cook. All a vast change to her spacious apartment in Sydney, but she wasn't going to dwell on the past. She was pleased not to be sharing her staircase and floor with anyone else.

"Would you like a cup of tea?" Pat asked. "Oh, but you're from Australia. Maybe you're used to coffee?"

Moira smiled. "We do drink a lot of coffee but I'll have a glass of water please."

Pat led the way to her lounge. While drinking her glass of water, Moira questioned Pat and found out that the rent was reasonable, she could move in that day and she was not tied to a contract. Only a week's notice was required when leaving. The rent included bed linen and towels; another saving. Pat also suggested she use washer and drier under the staircase. Moira was relieved to have a more comfortable and permanent home after four nights at the B&B. Living out of a suitcase had its challenges.

After finalising arrangements with Pat, the plan was that Moira check out of her B&B before midday and return with her suitcase and a month's payment in advance by about lunchtime. This was more seamless than her recent departure from her apartment in Sydney. In the afternoon she made friends with Pat's cottage by settling herself in, unpacking her suitcase and arranging her personal effects.

Later Moira sat in the wingchair and surveyed her scaled-down version of a home. Her unpacked clothes were hanging in the wardrobe. A framed photo of her family stood on the writing desk. She had managed to store her water colour and oil paints in one of the drawers of the desk. A vase of tulips stood on the window sill, a contrast to the emerald green silk curtains.

After being in the public eye during her move to the cottage in Main Street, Moira was not surprised that Zara James called to speak to her that afternoon. She said an emergency had arisen and asked whether Moira would like to work in the gallery that Saturday in return for a flat fee. Moira thought it was rather short notice but hoped it might lead to more work so she agreed.

"The gallery opens at 10:30 am and you'll lock up at 4:30 pm."

"What about the keys?"

"I'll drop them into your cottage this afternoon. I just want you to answer the phone, dust and hoover. If anyone wants to buy a painting place a red sticker on the painting and remember to write down the buyer's name, address and phone number. I have set up coffee facilities so help yourself."

Zara had a clipped way of pronouncing her words that made her sound curt. Moira found it at odds with her appearance.

Now that Moira had a permanent address, she was anxious to set up a bank account as soon as possible. If she hurried she would arrive before the NatWest branch in the village closed – Pat had said that was where to go.

That afternoon, Moira indulged herself in a long hot shower with some of the shower gel she must have thrown into her suitcase in Sydney at the last moment – she had no recollection of packing it, but was thankful for the familiar smell. As she rubbed in the gel, she appreciated she had at least established her roots in amenable surroundings. The extension of her visa for the UK was her next priority. It was only a week ago, last Friday, that she had farewelled some of her friends at a restaurant in Sydney, and so much had happened since then. She wondered how her resignation had been received at school the following Monday when lessons resumed after the holidays.

She woke up in the middle of the night feeling thirsty. Half-asleep, she reached out for the glass of water on her bedside table. A soft hand was what she felt. She whipped her hand back. Her heart began to beat faster. A tight knot formed in her chest. Was that a shadow against the white wall? She must be hallucinating or severely jet-lagged. The hairs on her arms were sticking up. Like a child, she buried herself under the comforting duvet. How foolish. She reached her hand out again. The same soft hand. Her breathing had now become shallow.

She swallowed hard, grabbed her pillow and waved it from side to side in front of her. Easing herself out of her bed, she was able to stretch her arm out to switch the light on. There was no one there. Yet the physical imprint of another hand was still with her.

She then noticed the curtain swinging. The window had been opened but it had been a still night. Still her heart was racing. She sat down on the bed and drank her water. Best to leave the light on. Sleep was slow in coming. Finally when it came, her dreams were about packing and repacking her suitcase endlessly. Her passport kept disappearing: whenever she had it in her hand, a spiteful wind blew it away.

Chapter 7

On Saturday morning, Moira opened up the gallery and completed the daily chores. The paintings sat well on the white wattle and daub walls in the fifteenth century cottage. The period look of the cottage enhanced the paintings. They would also sit well in classically decorated reception rooms.

Moira took time to study the paintings in the exhibition more closely. Felicity Green was a skilled water colourist but what was she trying to achieve as an artist? The subject matter in her exhibition was the West Sussex landscape, except for two still lifes which Moira considered superior in quality. Still lifes appealed to Moira as she believed they were more than just vases, fruit and cloths in some arrangement. She appreciated them as paintings of silence.

In the afternoon, the gallery was popular with visitors. Some of them wanted to chat about the technique used in the paintings, so she was able to call upon her knowledge of art. One elderly gentleman, presumably an art dilettante, wanted to philosophise.

"Although art reflects society, there's more to living than the contemporary consumer society," he said. "The feelings art expresses are essential to humanity; no liberal arts education, and a civilisation collapses."

She enjoyed the stimulation that this contact with people gave her and was glad she had studied the history of art in recent years.

After Moira closed up the gallery, she followed Scarlett's advice about protecting herself against the rain and went to the men's clothing shop where the waxed Barbour jackets were sold to both men and women. She was amazed that the traditional hip-length jackets sold at £80. Expensive. The serving lady asked her whether she wanted the detachable hood, which was astonishingly expensive, at £40. She was very conscious of the need to budget, but on the other hand, a jacket like this offered warmth and kept the rain out all year, so it was an investment. She bought both. Passing the electrical shop she decided to treat herself to a sandwich toaster as well.

In the afternoon as she stepped out of the gallery into Main Street, she saw a lanky man emerge from the School of English a few doors down. As he drew near her, he greeted her. "Aren't you the Moira who arrived from Australia a few days ago?"

News travelled fast in West Gidding.

"Yes, I'm Moira Capaldi." She shook hands. "Are you involved with the English School then?"

"I'm the Director, Tony Carter. You wouldn't be looking for some work, would you?" he said with a twinkle in his eye.

"Why do you ask?"

"I was only joking." His face crinkled with laughter, dimples appearing in his cheeks.

"I'm an experienced English teacher with an extra ESL qualification." Moira hoped her interest sounded low key.

"Well, we can talk about teaching. Make an appointment with the receptionist at the school."

"I have to confess I spoke to your receptionist early this week." Moira held her breath. "How was your trip to Brighton? Did the students enjoy the

Pavilion?"

"Yes, but I'm afraid I can't talk now. I need to meet some new arrivals and introduce them to their host families. I'll speak to you when you come in for your appointment."

A hands-on director.

That evening she sought out Pat to tell her about last night's *hand* experience. Pat listened attentively while Moira talked. Then she said, "You may be interested in hearing about my experience. When Gerard, my husband, and I first moved into this cottage, we lived in one part of the house with all our belongings while we worked with some outside help on the other parts."

"How long did this redecorating last?"

"The best part of two years, and that included only the basics. The cottage was in very poor condition. We left the latches on the original doors. We would go to bed and were woken up when the light went on and the door latch opened, usually about 2 am."

"Somehow I can believe that."

"We got the electrician to modernise the whole electrical system in the cottage. The door latches continued to open with lights coming on, but less frequently than when we moved in. As for your experience last night, I've no explanation for that. Would you like to move to another room in the cottage? I'm afraid I can't offer a separate bathroom with another bedroom."

"I'm fine. I will stay where I am."

"Do you know, we still have what was a powder room for men's wigs in the fifteenth century?" Her pride in this historical fact was evident in her face.

"No. How interesting."

"Yes, although we modernised the cottage to make it comfortable, it does have a history. West Gidding also has a historical society which can fill you in with details of its background."

Moira returned to her room and stood at the door pondering. A haunted house? What next? Village life revolved around a small group of people. Anyone with strong eccentricities would make relationships challenging.

She thought about Michael Upton. He had not been in contact again. Was he keeping her waiting? She mustn't make excuses for him. That had been her mistake with Guido. Just then the phone rang. It was Michael Upton. Telepathy.

"Hello, It's Mike. I hope you don't mind but I got your home phone number from Zara. How are you?"

Moira's throat was dry. She was well aware of the chemistry between them.

"Fine, thank you."

"I haven't forgotten our lunch. Is tomorrow still OK with you? We could go to a pub on the South Downs. Do you fancy a walk first?" He was persistent and she had her smart rainwear…

"Sure. I'd enjoy that," she replied.

He would collect her at 10:30 am. Was this a date?

On Sunday, Moira woke up and yawned,

stretching out her arms. She felt the room she was renting had been stamped with her personality; with her unpacked possessions around her, it felt like home. She tried to reassure herself that her lunch with Mike was not a proper date, and determined to enjoy the outing. It wasn't raining but she would still take her Barbour jacket just in case.

Not much later, Mike arrived in his BMW. Scarlett owned a Jensen Healey, and Mike a BMW. Ouch. Not having her own car hurt. Oh for the materially comfortable life in Australia… The air crackled between them. Moira was fiddling with her jacket cuffs, feeling awkward.

"Have you seen much of the South Downs?"

His words were enunciated as if he was making a speech in court.

"Since I got here last Monday I've only meandered around the village."

"What made you come to West Gidding?"

Moira considered how much she should reveal.

"I reached an executive position after working my way up the teaching ladder, but in the last four years art became my passion, and I visited Europe on trips to the famous galleries. I was also here last January, attending an art workshop."

"So no boyfriend left disappointed in Australia?" he said.

There was silence. She looked out of the window.

"I'm waiting for my divorce to come through."

Silence again. He could sense she was reticent about speaking about her personal life so he changed the subject.

"You were an air hostess at one stage?"

At that moment she thought of Scarlett's words of warning. News travelled fast in West Gidding.

"For a few years. What about you? You're a lawyer but what else do you do?"

"By coincidence, I'm keen on art too," he smiled. "I studied art a long time ago. Over the years I've experimented with all the media. I tend to use gouache or water colours opaquely. I particularly enjoy abstracting representational work."

She was being sucked into her favourite topic.

"Not oils?"

"When I have the time and space. Not recently. They take so long to dry."

"I like the style of the Impressionists, and brought all my oils with me, hoping to get plenty of chance to paint."

He chuckled. "We'll have to have a painting session together."

Moira did not respond. They had finally arrived in the parking space for walkers and she was ready to enjoy the scenery. They set off at a brisk pace. She soon realised Mike's long legs ate the miles, while she trotted behind him. This was not her style at all. She couldn't walk at his pace and conduct a conversation as well. In addition, her Barbour jacket weighed her down.

Forty-five minutes into the walk, the inevitable rain arrived, making further walking unsafe. For the first time, Moira found herself welcoming it, though she was aware rain would turn her hair into corkscrews. It was difficult to be glamorous in this climate.

"There's a pub nearby. Let's go and have a drink," Mike said.

She attempted to retain some grace, clambering down rocks, but Mike took her by her elbow and helped her. The pub was called *The Fox and Hound* and it had retained its period look inside, though a fresh coat of paint avoided a neglected appearance. Moira had seen so many pubs spoiled by so-called modernisation. A fire had been started up in an age-blackened fireplace. The bar was beginning to fill up, mainly with walkers caught in the rain. Mike went to collect the lagers. Moira was still finding it strange to drink non-refrigerated beer in England.

Once Mike seated himself on the sofa beside her, she was able to look into his eyes. Perhaps the blue shirt he was wearing brought out the blue of his eyes. He had style.

"So are you painting anything special now?" she said.

"Would you like to see my work?"

"That's not what I meant."

"But would you like to? You haven't answered

my question."

He was baiting her.

"Oh I see. As a lawyer you like to spar?"

His face broke into a smile as she relaxed enough to enjoy the game. She grinned in response. Her eyes sparkled. She shifted her position on the sofa.

"Let's order some food. Hot food, or just a sandwich?" His mellow tone of voice sounded caring.

"Let's see what's available on the blackboard."

Her decision was quick. Curry and rice. She felt around inside her handbag for some money but Mike was faster. He had ordered the food and paid for her.

Something stirred in Moira. A pang. A longing. A feeling she would like to push away. She wanted to erase the feeling of vulnerability Mike brought out in her. It was a long time since she had experienced a man caring for her, even on a superficial level. His actions made her confront her hidden feelings – anger and resentment.

"When did you start painting?" His soft, gentle voice broke through her ruminations.

"About four years ago."

She was hesitant to start talking about her art. It had replaced her teaching in importance, and had become a way of expressing her feelings. She wasn't sure she wanted to share her real thoughts.

"I went to an art exhibition, liked what I saw, but thought I could do as well, if not better. Little did I then know what painting involved: composition, colour theory, tone, perspective..." Her tone was light and she laughed.

"I enrolled in a Life Class and to practise my drawing skills. It was like daring myself to achieve on a level other than logical," Mike said.

"I felt the same."

"Have you ever tried abstracting your drawings in paint?"

"I don't know how to do that."

"Come on. It's not difficult. It's another way of perceiving the environment."

"But I like the Impressionists."

"They are like mush."

He was a lawyer and would always aim to win

an argument. Moira shrugged her shoulders. As much as she would never have admitted it to Mike, she was enjoying herself.

"Do you cook for yourself?"

Moira helped herself to some more chicken curry.

"You ask a lot of questions."

"Just getting to know you."

"In that case keep going. I do enjoy cooking a dinner for friends. Of course it depends on whether I have time." He paused, "You're not leading up to an invitation, are you?"

"If you say so," she laughed.

They had almost finished eating their lunch. Engrossed in each other, they hadn't noticed the bar filling up, but the background noise was starting to intrude on their conversation.

"Shall we go?" said Mike.

Reluctantly she rose from the armchair.

"I'd like to take you to the bluebells near Billingshurst now."

They made their way back to the car. Bluebells

as piercing as the blue of his eyes; how appropriate.When they arrived at the woods near Billingshurst, Moira was moved by the sight. She breathed in the intense, sweet scent. It was so powerful it cleansed her nasal passages and moved to her brain, converting muddled thinking into clarity. The thousands of bluebells merged together like waves and gave the impression of vibrating, beneath the solidity of established trees. The sun played hide and seek amongst the canopy, filtering through the branches, creating shafts of light and appearing to shimmer over the bluebells. She was grateful for the silence. Time passed. Her awareness of Mike standing beside her increased the emotional intensity of the sharing. Then a distant cuckoo pierced the air, its sound breaking the silence.

Slowly, Moira emerged from her reverie and heard Mike starting the engine. The car slid off into the quiet of the deserted road in the woodlands. They both preferred to avoid chatting for the rest of the journey. When they arrived at her cottage all she managed was, “Thank you very much. Much appreciated, Mike."

She looked into his eyes. He pressed the back of her hand to his lips. They both understood the shared moment.

That night Scarlett rang to confirm their walking arrangement for Wednesday.

"So have you got rain gear?"

"I bought a Barbour jacket."

"Good for you."

"But I've no walking boots yet."

"What size do you wear?"

"An English six."

"Oh we're into the English sizes," Scarlett laughed amicably. "Don't worry. I'll bring a pair that size. You'll enjoy the South Downs a lot more if your feet are well-protected. See you soon."

Alone and uninterrupted, Liz was sitting in the staff room, preparing lessons during a spare period. A peremptory knock broke into her concentration, and she rose to open the door. A good looking man with a photogenic face leaned against the door frame. Parents were supposed to go to reception at the main entrance, but before she could tell him so, the man said,

"Sorry to bother you. Is Moira at school today?"

She figured out this must be Guido. Softly spoken, he seemed to be ill-at-ease but she couldn't invite him into the staffroom. She closed the door behind her and joined him in the corridor. "You must be Guido."

"Yes."

"I'm afraid Moira hasn't come back this term." She hesitated whether to continue, but his face showed strain and lack of sleep. "Moira has resigned from teaching."

Guido's eyes opened wider in disbelief. He stared at Liz.

"I don't know any more," Liz lied.

Guido thanked her and left abruptly, without saying another word.

Later during lunchtime she overheard those

who had attended the Doyle's farewell for Moira, commenting on Guido's surreptitious jaunt through the school in search of his wife.

"Does he know Moira has left for the UK?" someone said. The yells from the playground echoed around the staffroom.

"I don't think so," whispered Liz, "and more's the pity."

Chapter 8

On Tuesday, Moira was on duty at the gallery. She was completing the chores when the twinkle of the doorbell startled her. Whirling her head round, she caught sight of a short man entering, his blonde hair tousled by the wind. His bushy eyebrows met in the middle of his corrugated forehead. His good looks had faded with age, and the pink scalp shone through the balder patches. His black woollen coat, which had seen better times, reached down to his ankles and kept tripping him up. A prospective buyer? Surely not.

"Good morning," she said. "How are you?"

"What is it to you?" a gravelly voice responded.

To say she was ill-at-ease was an understatement. English people were always polite, so why was he being so rude to her? Perhaps he was too class-conscious. In Australia, everyone was equal, except perhaps for people who were snobbish about money. Well, she was here to serve clients.

"Would you like some coffee?"

He snorted.

"Let's go out for a coffee."

Moira was startled at the suggestion. Was he flirting with her?

"Sorry, I can't leave the gallery unattended."

"Why not? You haven't got many people looking at the moment. No one will know. You can tell Zara Edward called."

"That's not the point."

"Are you afraid of Zara?"

She gasped at his impudence. He flicked his blonde mane out of his eyes. The phone rang, breaking the pregnant silence. It was an enquiry about opening times.

"We are closed on Mondays and Sundays," she said.

Her eyes followed his movements as he circulated around the gallery space. As she put the phone down, he stomped out through the front door. Still flustered by his rudeness, she opened her mouth to say goodbye, but he was already in the street.

As she was locking the gallery front door that afternoon, she heard a cheerful, "Hello".

It was Tony Carter. He adjusted his tie.

"You haven't come over to the school to tell me about your teaching."

It sounded as if Tony might be interested in employing her.

"Would 2 pm tomorrow suit you?" said Moira.

"Super. I'll look forward to it," said Tony, and disappeared.

Moira remembered she needed documents for the visa. A call to her father would be necessary, to tap into his meticulous records. Pat suggested she keep costs down by ringing at an off-peak time, so later in the evening, Moira used her international phone card. Her parents' phone rang for a long time. Disappointed and puzzled, she put the receiver down; she had timed the call to catch them at 8 am Australia time, they couldn't possibly be out at that time of the morning.

Next day, she let herself out of the cottage into the cool air to walk. Eventually she came to the building that housed the West Gidding Historical

Society. A qualified volunteer historian was on duty. Moira broached the subject of number 36.

"That cottage was originally a coach house for the Manor House, but for a while the servants were housed there while the Manor was being extended. When they were returned to the servants' quarters in the Manor house, the coach house became empty."

"Did number 36 ever have a name?"

"Yes. It was named after the Lord of the Manor, so *Penfold Cottage*."

"Is there any history of ghosts?"

"There have been rumours over the years that his wife, Lady Penfold, a woman educated in music and literature, haunted the cottage. In those days of arranged marriages, she was forced to marry wealthy Lord Penfold, a man twice her age, which brought money to her parents. As a woman she was disempowered. Later she fell in love with a man below her station and they would meet in the former coach house, Pat's present cottage. This all ended when Lord Penfold discovered what was happening and made it his business to remove the lover."

"How sad."

"No one knew what had happened. Her lover disappeared. People speculated that the lover had been killed by Lord Penfold. In any case, Lady Penfold was heartbroken. Now some people feel the cottage is haunted."

That didn't surprise Moira.

"Make what you will of the story…"

Moira spent the rest of the morning locating her certificates and degree documents, before attending her interview at the School of English. The receptionist introduced herself as Penelope Baxter and suggested Moira go to Tony's office upstairs. The rooms she could see through open doorways were bigger than the ones in the cottages, although Tony had told her he kept his classes small. Moira took her time climbing the stairs.

"Hello, do sit down. Cup of coffee?" said Tony. "Gallery work is a change of career for you surely?" He rang Penny for the coffees to be brought up.

"Yes, but it's fun compared to what I used to do.

Here are my degree and teaching diploma documents."

Tony skimmed through them.

"So, tell me about your teaching in Sydney."

"I taught English literature to students from fourteen to eighteen years of age. Later, I completed a postgraduate course which enabled me to teach ESL students. I then pioneered programmes for top Chinese students taking matriculation for entry into Australian universities."

"So you were dealing with older students."

"In later years, yes. I enjoyed this work most of all."

"That's super. What we offer here are courses for all levels of speaking and writing English. Nothing as formal as your experience, but the students come from all over the world. Some teenagers come each year during holidays, and some come for blocks of two or three months. I have no problems in finding staff to cover most of these contingencies." Tony tidied the documents she had handed to him. "What I'm finding these days is that businessmen from Europe, frequently from Germany, want to polish up their business English skills, and they require a completely different approach. They are often short of time, so they take three-day-weekends, or come for five days in a row. Would you be willing to take some of them on?"

"Yes, I'd like to work with them. How big are your classes?"

"You will work with students on a one-to-one basis. As they have to take time out from their business schedules, their arrivals are erratic and spread throughout the year. Often last minute arrangements are made."

"Thanks for thinking of me."

"I would be paying you by the hour, £10 an hour."

Moira swallowed hard. The payment per hour was higher than what she received from Zara.

"I hope you will join our teaching team."

"I've started the ball rolling in London regarding my permanent residency situation. I'm waiting for some documents to arrive from Sydney," she said.

"If you get caught up in the government bureaucratic process, I have some contacts with the Home Office. I often have to deal with visas of for foreign students coming from Japan, Malaysia and so on. Just let me know."

She wished she had known this earlier.

That evening she tried calling her parents again. As the phone started to ring, she crossed her fingers. Her father answered. *Thank goodness.*

"Hi Pa. How are you? I'm so sorry to be ringing so early. I need your help with documents for my UK residency. I was wondering whether you still had your British passport or any documents or letters to prove we had lived in the UK, or when we left?"

"Ohh...that was such a long time ago. I don't know what I have. I'd have to look in my records file. Are you keeping well?"

"Yes. Things are settling down. I've found a place to rent, rooms in a fifteenth century cottage. Some teaching may come my way, and I do a little reception work at an art gallery. Can I speak to Ma?"

"She's in the shower."

"OK. Must go. I'll ring back in a day or two. Love to you and Ma. Byeee."

That evening she was settling into bed when she heard a clicking noise. Clickety, clackety. The sound was in her room. She recalled the evening with the hand, and felt a prickling sensation up her spine. Finally she got out of bed and tried to figure out where the sound was located. It was coming from the wall opposite the window. Extraordinary. It was time to stop being so nervous about her historical cottage. She searched in her cabin bag for her faithful friends, her ear plugs, and clambered into bed but she kept her bedside light on once again.

On the Wednesday of the proposed walk with Scarlett, the sunny weather was replaced by rain moving in from the East. Moira tried to compose herself in readiness for a rainy afternoon. When Scarlett arrived in a jaunty jacket with fake fur collar, the downpour of rain had been replaced by gentle showers.

"Do you know Felicity Green? I've got the gallery brochure but do you know anything more personal about her?"

"I've never met her, which is unusual, because we all get to know one another in such a small community. I do know she belongs to the London-based Royal Water Colour Society, which demands a high standard of water colour painting. I missed her last exhibition opening at the West Gidding Gallery. I know she's married with no children."

"Thanks. That's interesting," Moira smiled, then her tone changed. "I did some work in the gallery yesterday and I had a beastly man come into the gallery this week. He went out of his way to be rude."

"I bet it was Edward Wishbone. He's a newcomer to West Gidding, and seems to be a loner. He's brewing a nice reputation for being ill mannered, but he's very good looking isn't he?"

Apparently Edward had been a talented artist

with a promising future. He had trained in London at the Slade. Then he met a woman. They fell in love, got married, six weeks later it was over. He lost money to her, which unhinged him mentally. Then he found out that the law required him to wait a few years for the divorce.

"What a life. I've seen him at a few art exhibitions in local towns such as Henfield and Petworth," continued Scarlett. "At one stage, he was rumoured to be having an affair with Zara." Scarlett was locking up her car. "Did you know that Zara had escaped from Yugoslavia? She lived in London for a while before settling in West Sussex."

"Really. She would have had a difficult time then."

Moira was looking forward to walking in the South Downs again this time fully equipped with her gear designed to protect her from the steady drizzle. Scarlett parked her car, and said, "The widows from around West Gidding are getting very curious about Edward's marital status. So, are you interested in him?" Scarlett prompted with a sly grin.

"Are you joking? No way. I don't need men with problems. I have enough of my own."

"You know after our conversation over dinner last week, I wondered whether you ever thought of leaving your husband?"

"I often thought about leaving him, but the logistics bewildered me for various reasons. I wasn't sure what decision to take, so I procrastinated. These days when I can't make a decision, I just let everything go, and eventually circumstances, or call it Fate, take over. Events then push me into making decisions which become obvious."

"And you didn't speak to your parents about him?"

"My mother was of the generation who put her children before her personal happiness but I didn't feel she would understand my position. My sister had settled in the US, my brother was still travelling around the world as a freelance photographer, so I felt I had to solve my own problems."

"And then?"

"Eventually I accepted Guido wasn't going to

change, and that coincided with the time my teaching career blossomed with new opportunities opening up, so I began to focus on my project at school. By then we were leading separate lives; it became a relationship where we remained together out of sheer convenience."

"And after that?"

"In the last few years we only shared one meal a week. In recent years as my teaching job became more routine I got involved with art courses and they grew on me,"

"Are you divorcing him then?"

"Yes. I saw a lawyer before I left Australia and instructed him to start divorce proceedings, which would also include the sale of our apartment. Moira frowned. "I haven't been in touch with Guido since I left my note in the apartment."

"Life is so complicated."

They had been so absorbed in their conversation they hadn't noticed the rain had stopped and now the sun was emerging.

"Look at the rainbow," Moira said. They both

stopped in their tracks to admire the colours, breathing in the fresh air, and stretching themselves as if to free themselves from any angst. They both felt healthily tired.

"Do you fancy going to the pub to finish off the day?"

Scarlett threw her red raincoat into the boot of her car. Red was obviously a favourite colour of hers but then her name *was* Scarlett. Moira nodded her head. They drove to a pub outside West Gidding, ordered some lager and found a table outside in the garden. No sooner had they sat down than a now-familiar voice boomed out,

"Enjoying your day?" It was Tony and it looked as if he and an entire cricket team were quenching their thirst.

"Well ladies, I hope you are free on Saturday. The school is having a disco in the local community hall." Tony seemed pleased, so they must have won their match.

"So you think we might qualify as students of English?" teased Scarlett.

"The students will be attending but this time we are inviting people from outside the school as well. Sort of mixing up folks."

"Does that mean the music will be too loud to talk?"

"Come on Scarlett. You're not so old. It will be fun."

"Casual dress?" asked Moira. Her problem with clothes in the UK was that stylish clothes had to be covered up with unattractive jackets, in case of rain.

"Yes. We'll be holding a barbecue in the grounds of the hall. We've booked a tent just in case. People will be able to sit down, eat, drink and talk between dances in the hall. Hopefully see you Saturday," and he sidled off.

"It'll be an opportunity for you to meet some locals, Moira."

"So might we see more of Edward Wishbone?"

"No, I don't think the art world will be there." Scarlett was rummaging in her handbag looking for some lipstick. "Ohh," she cried out. "So sorry. I forgot to give you a letter which arrived from

Australia for you yesterday. I was going to give it to you as soon as I arrived. My memory is getting worse."

Moira reached out for the letter. She recognized her mother's writing. She pocketed it, intending to read it at the cottage later.

Chapter 9

As soon as Moira had reached her bedroom, she ripped the envelope to read the letter. Was it going to be a lecture? She wondered whether her father would have anything to say; her parents rarely agreed on anything. Her eyes returned to the beginning of the letter. It was written two days after her birthday

My Dearest Moira

Belated birthday wishes to you. Your present has gone by separate mailing and will arrive after this letter. You have been in our thoughts a lot.

Guido rang us a few days after we received your letter. He asked us if we knew where you were. I said no. He rang again wanting your address. Don't worry, we won't pass it on.

You did what was right for you. We're both glad you had the courage to take this step. Guido was the one who was selfish in his approach to life. We both agree you would have destroyed yourself if you had stayed in the marriage.

It was much better you wrote a note instead of facing him, otherwise you would have had to deal with drama, abuse, tears and so on.

I feel pity for Guido. He'll be lost without you but I imagine your life will now flourish. For your sake I hope so.

Do fill us in with news about your "new life".

Love from us both

Ma

Strong words. Moira felt the cold spread to her outer limbs. Her mother wrote they thought she would have destroyed herself; had they seen through the walls she had built to protect herself? Her parents only met Guido on the odd occasion, Christmas or a wedding, as she and Guido had always lived in a different city from her family. Her mother had used the word *abuse* and she wondered how far they had speculated. She sat down at the writing desk and unscrewed her fountain pen. A short résumé of her activities, and her new address would do the trick.

Monday found her waking up late, ensconced in the comfort of her bed. The letter lay on her bedside table. It felt good to have established contact with her parents, especially as they approved of her actions. She felt like staying in bed longer, yet nagging thoughts niggled at her. She had to write the letter to the Police Constabulary in Edinburgh to check if the police had any record of her family living in Scotland. She also had to ring the government department dealing with National Insurance numbers. It was better to attend to that as soon as possible. A brunch later this morning would replace breakfast. She wrote out a draft or her letter, and then rewrote it, altering it slightly. Postage would have to be first class.

Moira took advantage of her jaunt to the shops to buy a pair of comfortable walking boots at the Barbour shop.

When she returned to number 36, it took her some time to get through to the right Police department by phone. The second official pointed out that the Home Office required proof that she had lived in Scotland first, only then would they be prepared to make the long, arduous search through their records. So she was back to square one. She was used to being in control, but her situation demanded dependency on others, and that left her feeling uncomfortable. She was frustrated and bored with the process.

In the evening she made another call to her parents. This time Moira was ready with her notes from the Home Office.

"So how is my Moira? I have my British passport, but it has expired. I have some documents given to us on our departure as well as my appointment letter."

"Super. Could you could send all these documents by registered mail please? The address is ..." the phone line started to crackle.

"I can't hear you." Her father had poor hearing, and the hearing aid would often interfere with the phone conversation.

"Don't worry Pa. I'll ring later."

She turned round after the call and saw Pat in the process of leaving the cottage.

"I'm glad I caught you. I heard a strange noise in my room. It was louder than a cricket but definitely a clicking noise. It was coming from a wall, would you believe."

Pat's face crinkled as she laughed aloud.

"My dear, that's a death-watch beetle. They often burrow in old buildings. Don't worry about it," she said and tripped out of the cottage. After her experience with the mysterious hand, Moira was uncertain whether it was that simple.

She decided to ring her parents again, and as before, her father picked up the phone.

"Pa, have you got a pen handy?"

"Yes, pet." This time the line was devoid of crackling.

"The address for the documents is c/o Pat Myles, 36 Main Street, West Gidding, West Sussex BN44 2HL, UK."

"You will return them to me when you are finished, won't you?" said her father.

Her parents were fanatical about holding on to their documents, expired or not. Maybe she should follow their example.

"Of course, Pa. Tell Ma I was happy to hear from her."

What a relief to have her father sending the documents at last. After the call, feeling raw, she retired to her quarters, and solitude. The innocent phone call to Pa was reminding her of a life where the essentials of living, job, money and home, were taken for granted. She curled up on her bed and emptied her mind with yoga breathing.

Mike was having a difficult dinner, attempting to end his relationship with Margaret. He had taken her to a smart restaurant and told her he had fallen in love with a woman he had met.

At first, Margaret asked him, "Who is it?"

"She's recently arrived here from Australia." No point in giving her too much fuel for gossip.

"How recently?" Margaret asked, sharply.

"A week ago."

"If you've just met her, it's early days." Margaret pushed the food around her plate with a fork.

"What is she doing here?"

"She's settling in West Gidding." Mike was starting to be irritated by the questioning.

"It's a case of ships passing in the night," she said, confidently. "Nothing will come of it."

Then out of the blue, Margaret's face crinkled in anger. She spat out,

"Don't give me that crap. You have led me into believing we had a future together and now you want to back out."

Mike's feelings curdled in the face of the venomous attack. He was riveted to the spot. Her raised voice had attracted the attention of other diners, and he realised he had made a mistake. Margaret considered his openness as weakness.

"Would you like anything else to eat," he asked.

"How do you expect me to have any appetite to eat after what you said?" she mocked.

"In that case, I will take you home," he said, standing up decisively.

In the afternoon before the disco, Moira found

herself napping on the bed. She was tired; apparently the combination of jet lag and life changes was draining. She covered the dark circles under her eyes with make-up and looked at her meagre collection of clothes. Black slacks and a red top were not exciting but would have to do, as her choice of clothing was limited. The one woollen jumper that she had brought from Australia would keep her warm if she sat outside. She enjoyed the fact that daylight lasted till about 9 pm, but found the evening temperatures chilly. There was always her new Barbour jacket, if it did rain. She disliked her dressing style being hampered by the chance of rain. When Scarlett called for her at 7 pm, she looked glamorous, as usual, in an exotic turquoise blouse she had bought in Florence, and white slacks; a navy jacket over her arm. She was good company for the soul, with her light-hearted comments. They drew up at the community centre where only a few cars were parked. The students had put up coloured lights outside but these would be lit later when darkness replaced daylight. Taped disco music was being played inside the hall until the live band arrived at 8 pm.

The smell of onions, steak and sausages signalled that the cooking had already started on the barbecue. Glasses of beer were being siphoned off from the barrel. They paid for their tickets and made their way inside the tent where tables and chairs had been set up. Tony was nowhere to be seen.

Moira sensed that Scarlett was eager to talk, and sure enough, once they were seated, Scarlett began. “I have some news. Nick and I have started talking about separating.”

“Who initiated the subject?”

“It all happened after our walk on Sunday. We had gone to see a film, a rare occurrence for us. The main theme of the film was the disintegration of a couple’s relationship. I asked Nick what he thought went wrong between the characters, as a way of addressing relationship issues without playing the blame game in our own.”

“And then?”

“It led to the two of us questioning whether it was possible for things to be improved in the film situation. The argument which resulted went around in circles, and sadly we switched to our personal life and hurtful words were uttered."

"That's a pity. Maybe there was a backlog of resentment that needed to be aired?"

"Maybe. But then we didn't talk for a couple of days. Nick accused me of being provocative. I wanted to leave him there and then, but luckily I spoke to my lawyer who said if I left home now I would lose my ownership rights to shared belongings and property. He advised we both negotiate a legal separation through our lawyers."

"So what are you going to do?"

Just then Tony sauntered over to ask Moira to dance. What a pity to be interrupted. Once they entered the hall, she saw how well the students had done with their decorating. Red crêpe paper adorned the fluorescent lights, creating a nightclub atmosphere. The band was swinging away under pulsating lights which they had brought; old and young were gyrating to the disco rhythms. Moira and Tony joined the crowd on the dance floor. It was a long time since she had danced, but she enjoyed herself, and was even introduced to some of the local teachers during the pauses between dance numbers. The body heat had built up in the hall, making the cooler temperatures outside feel refreshing.

On returning to her table outside, she found Scarlett had been asked to dance, so Tony sat down, a warm beer in his hand. Moira took a sip of her wine.

"How often do you have these discos?" she asked.

"About every three weeks; often enough for them to communicate in English."

"Do you ever have undesirable incidents taking place?"

"Occasionally we have students who drink too much, but we just remove the offenders from the hall and drive them home."

At that point Scarlett was escorted back to her table.

"We try to prevent such incidents by giving a short pep talk beforehand."

Tony excused himself and went off to check on

the students. Moira recalled how teachers never relaxed at such events. She was glad to be out of that scene these days. They collected their portions of sizzling barbecued steak and helped themselves to salad. Moira unfolded her paper napkin.

"So what now?"

"We have both agreed to work on a legal separation. Nick's in therapy to help him cope. I think he would prefer no change, but sees no point in staying with me if I want to leave."

Just then Moira looked up. Her stomach began to churn: Mike Upton had arrived with a woman on his arm. In fact she was clutching, no, almost clawing at his arm. She was blonde, bottle-blonde, and she wore a light tweed skirt and jacket with a cream silk blouse. The clothes were too formal for a barbecue. They approached a neighbouring table, and Mike nodded in recognition but kept his distance.

Moira continued her conversation with Scarlett, but her eyes kept flitting to Mike and his partner every so often.

"I don't want to deliberately hurt Nick," said

Scarlett, "but separation is a step towards getting a divorce. It gives us both time to get used to the idea."

"And your heart?"

"My love for him has been eroded by familiarity and boredom. Nick's not participating in the relationship so I feel it's right to leave him. He's aging rapidly and wants to be left in peace. On another level, I'm already missing what I'm giving up. You know, the sense of security and home comforts. I also don't know how I'll cope with living alone."

"It's going to be a challenging time for you, a time when friends are important."

Her conversation with Scarlett was interrupted by further invitations to dance. At midnight the disco ended, but a lot of the students were just warming up. Some decided to visit a disco club in Brighton, but Scarlett and Moira went home. Moira was left with a sour taste in her mouth, and wishing she wasn't going out to lunch with Mike the next day.

When she got home, she found a light had been left on for her. She trudged up the stairs to her room. On her bedside table lay a pale blue envelope with red and blue diagonal lines at the edges. Another air mail letter from Australia; Liz Curtis this time.

My Dear Moira

I'm writing this at school so it's a quickie.

By third period on the first Monday back at school, I asked our new Principal, Rod Brown, if he had heard anything about you. He hadn't.

"She's left her job to pursue her artistic talents in England," I said.

"Is she happy?" was the first thing he said. Can you believe he puts personal happiness as no 1 in life?

Later we found out that the "efficient" public servant at Head Office had misplaced your resignation so all one hundred staff didn't know what had happened. You should have heard the different versions of what you had allegedly done... at least the three of us we were able to talk about you to each other.

It took Head Office another two days to find the form. The Principal couldn't employ a new teacher to replace you until Head Office found your resignation and processed it. The English Department was in chaos all this time.

Guido has dropped in on all your friends he knows. One day he came to the school asking whether you were there. He looked strained.

Mary had the forethought to clear your desk and we've split your books between ourselves.

I like your meditation tapes. Thought I'd keep them for myself. Maybe I'll get up and leave one of these days myself! We all miss you and frequently imagine you sitting at your easel painting. Think of us slaving away at school.

Take care and much love

Liz

P.S. Write soon!!!

She reread the contents of the letter again. Trust Liz to see the hilarious side of life. She chuckled to herself and relaxed.

Rod had originally caused a stir when he was the first gay to be appointed Principal to her Girls

High School, and perhaps because of this he tended to keep a low profile, publicly. She never questioned the appointment. As an air hostess in the pre-jumbo days, she used to be the only air hostess among a male crew of ten, many of whom were gays. They were always so considerate and helpful.

What puzzled Moira was how easily her friends in Australia accepted her decision to leave Guido. Did they see something she was missing? Indeed, what was her blind spot in relationships?

Chapter 10

Pat had gone to visit her family in Devon, and Moira removed herself from the outside world by spending Thursday morning catching up on chores such as washing and ironing. Later, she felt more in the mood for writing letters and updating her parents and friends on her latest activities. Moira was enjoying her solitude, when Tony called at the cottage.

"Glad you're in. I've received a letter from a German businessman who wants to come for English lessons all next week. Interested?" He lifted his eyebrows in a double movement as if urging her to say *yes*.

"I'd be delighted to teach him."

Moira liked Tony's easy-going manner. All the village people were polite and welcoming, maybe too much so. There was a danger the local community could become too incestuous, full of gossip, and a real contrast to her more anonymous life in Sydney.

The phone rang. Her heart fluttered at the sound

of Mike's voice. He invited her to go to London with him the following Saturday and visit the Tate Gallery. Moira jumped at the chance to see the latest exhibition and they agreed on a time for a pick up. On their walk he had told her he usually went with a group of friends, and they factored in a meal as well. It sounded as if this time it was going to be a one-to-one. She wondered what had happened to the bottle-blonde companion from the barbecue.

That week also introduced Moira to another facet of life in West Sussex. She was working at the gallery again when a middle aged woman hobbled in. Unpretentious in appearance, she was leaning on a walking stick, eminently suitable for exploring the South Downs. "This ankle is such a nuisance," she said muttered. "I sprained it three months ago, and I still have problems with it."

"Would you like a coffee?"

"When I finish looking at the paintings. Thank you."

A woman who knew what she wanted. An independent woman. Moira pretended to be sorting out papers but discreetly watched the lady studying the paintings. She was taking her time. Good; she either knew all about water colours or was enjoying the paintings.

"I haven't seen you here before," she said as she shuffled around the gallery.

"I've recently come over from Australia."

"I have a daughter living in Cremorne in Sydney. I visited her last year. Lovely suburb near the harbour. So what are you doing in West Sussex?"

"I hope to settle here."

"Welcome to our parts. I will now accept your offer of a coffee. Black please. I will sit down and look at the paintings as I talk." Her sharp eyes continued to scan the content of the paintings. "So, how are you settling in?" she asked.

There would be a sale but it would be on the lady's terms, Moira gauged.

"I've found a suitable place to rent and am delighted to be working in this gallery. I also hope to find the time to paint myself."

"So you're a painter?"

“Not a professional one. I have spent my life teaching English, but I love to paint. It’s a good counterpoint to the logical activity of my brain.”

“Oh, you mean you are using the right hand side of your brain for art, and the left hand side of the brain for thinking.”

“So, you know all about that?” Moira laughed.

“Yes. By the way I’m Lady Allthorpe, but call me Elizabeth.”

“And I’m Moira Capaldi.”

“I want to buy a painting as a wedding present. Personally I prefer abstracts with lots of colour. I think this climate of ours deprives us of colour. However, people generally identify with the area they live in so I have decided to go for a safe choice, the painting of the South Downs.”

As Moira took out a red spot to place beside the painting indicated, Lady Allthorpe said,

“I presume a cheque is fine. Here are my details,” as Moira took out the receipt book, “and keep the business card.”

“We’ll phone you La... Elizabeth when the

exhibition ends, and arrange a time for you to pick up the painting."

"A pleasure dealing with you." She limped her way out into the street.

Her first sale. Zara would be pleased. Moira was left to her thoughts. English people wore a mask of politeness behind which the real individual lurked, such a contrast to the direct openness of Australians.

Life was moving forward. This week would be Moira's teaching week with the German businessman. Much of her life in England until now had been spent on integrating changes: setting up a place to live in, finding employment that would give her an income, and sorting out her visa. Living in a typical English village was different to life in a large cosmopolitan city, so she relished the thought of returning to something familiar, something that she was experienced at: her teaching.

When she arrived at the English school, Tony was chatting with Dieter, who seemed to be at ease with conversational English. He was a stout man of medium height, with greying hair at the temples and a blustery manner, but Moira felt comfortable with him. Tony escorted them to a room downstairs which seemed more like a sitting room. It housed two comfortable armchairs, as well as a table and chairs. A jug of water and glasses stood in readiness for the morning's session.

Moira began the session by quizzing Dieter about his background, his work and his expectations for the week. Dieter was not backward in talking about himself. His English was fluent and she mentally noted the few mistakes he had made so she could plan remedial work for later on. He lived with his family in a small village, but commuted to Frankfurt where he worked for an engineering company. After a coffee break, they moved to the table where she was ready to assess some of Dieter's written work, such as business letter writing skills.

When she completed her first day's teaching, Tony was working on administration in his office.

"How did you get on? A bit different to your Chinese students I expect?"

"Fine. He's a very conscientious student. I've pretty well worked out the programme which will serve him best, so I hope he'll find the week useful." As an afterthought she said, "and an enjoyable one."

"Let's go to the pub. You need to relax."

She picked up her papers and they ambled to *The Norfolk Arms.* It was a modern, functional pub with tacky plastic chairs and tables. There were three pubs in West Gidding, each establishment catering for a slightly different clientele, but the *Norfolk* was the nearest.

Once seated with their half pints of beer, Tony began with, "I am curious to hear more about your Chinese students."

Aware she sounded a little like a brochure, Moira explained, "Sydney, and other state capitals in Australia accepted the top Chinese students from the matriculation exam results in Malaysia. My girls' school took twenty students. They had all attended English-speaking schools and wanted to enter Australian universities to pursue medicine, optometry or higher mathematics. A pass in English was mandatory. At our school they spent one year completing the courses Australian students did in two years."

"Amazing application."

Something of a technical discussion on relative merits of international education systems and study habits of young people ensued, and by the time their drinks were finished, the pub was filled to capacity, and reverberating with tongues unravelled by the pints of beer which were being swigged.

"I'm off for a walk now. I need to stretch my legs after sitting all day."

After a couple of beers she needed to clear her head. She couldn't understand why Tony was so interested in the Chinese students.

Tony and she related as colleagues rather than as director and staff member. They were about the same age. Sometimes he would quiz her about her teaching ideas. She enjoyed Tony's dry sense of humour and his amiable nature. There was no artifice, just honesty. He was a good raconteur, and she felt jollied by his turn of phrase. His company felt as comfortable as putting on a well-worn pair of slippers, with nothing of the excitement of the forbidden that she encountered with Mike.

As the week progressed, Moira fell into the teaching pattern of 10 am to 5 pm. She and Dieter took an hour off for lunch, and short breaks for coffee. She felt her years of experience helped her introduce the work in an appealing way. She introduced magazines and newspapers for idiom practice in the afternoons, and Tony had a well-stocked library of videos to choose from for more sophisticated listening practice.

At the end of the week, Penny took a phone call from Pat at school with a message for Moira. A parcel from Australia had been delivered and signed for. Would Moira want it dropped off at the school?

Moira hesitated. She didn't like using work time for private matters but her relief at the arrival of documents overruled propriety. She wanted to check what papers were enclosed and make an appointment with Mary Reid at the Home Office as soon as possible.

“Yes please.”

Her dogged teaching application was transformed into a burst of enthusiasm to take another trip to London. She would schedule it for the following Monday.

“The documents have arrived from Australia,” Moira gloated to Tony. At the same time Pat rushed into the school with the slim package but couldn’t stay to chat. Moira’s patience was tested as she had to wait till the morning break to open it. She snipped the string round the brown paper; at least it wasn’t sealed with wax. Her father had sent his expired British passport which documented her as his child, his letter of appointment to the South Australian State Department as well as details of the ship journey the family took to Australia.

During the break, after a few phone call attempts, she was able to speak with Mary Reid, explaining that the documents from her father had arrived.

“I won’t be here on a Monday though you can speak to my replacement. If you want to see me, come on Wednesday at 10 am."

"Thank you, I will."

Her documents were a priority.

"Ring me if your plans change."

"Yes, of course."

After completing lessons for the morning, she used her lunchtime to complete photocopying the documents her father had sent her in Tony's office.

At the end of the week when Tony handed her an envelope full of pound notes, she clapped her hands and felt free to express her childlike excitement. She didn't care what he thought of her impetuous reaction. A significant sum of money coming to her was most welcome at this time – she would enjoy depositing it in her bank account.

"Do you know that you can choose to be registered as a self-employed taxpayer with spasmodic earnings in the UK? If you don't earn over the tax free allowance you won't have to pay any tax."

"Thanks for the tip. I'll have to appoint you as my financial adviser."

They both laughed. As she left the school, she became aware she was becoming fond of the school, or was it Tony she was fond of...?

She returned to the cottage to have a shower and change. The cottage front doorbell interrupted her plans. To her surprise there was Dieter holding a bunch of roses.

“To a very helpful teacher. I improved my English a lot. Thank you,” he said bowing slightly as he handed over the bouquet.

Her eyes warmed up to his act of kindness as she smiled and thanked him. She felt satisfied with her teaching week.

On Saturday Moira snuggled under the duvet. She was going to bring her breakfast to bed this morning. She had plenty of time before readying herself for the outing to the Tate Gallery. She checked its location in her London book of maps, searching for Millbank, an area she wasn’t familiar with. The Tate had been founded in 1897 as the National Gallery of British Art and was renamed the Tate

Gallery in 1932. Now it was a national collection of British and international, modern and contemporary art. She wondered what the difference might be between *modern* and *contemporary*. The year before it had introduced the controversial Turner Prize, open to British artists, or artists working in Britain, all under the age of fifty. Moira's visits to galleries in Paris, Vienna and Rome had embraced traditional art and the Impressionists. She surmised Mike hoped to extend her knowledge of abstraction today, after all, she had admitted ignorance on that subject during the walk on the South Downs.

Armed with her umbrella, Moira waited for Mike outside Zara's gallery. Mike arrived on time and got out of the BMW to greet her. His business suit was replaced by smart casual trousers and cashmere sweater, and he exuded sophistication and sartorial elegance. A kerchief round his neck seemed to be his contribution to the art theme for the day. As he leaned over to take her jacket, the scent of her perfume fused with his cologne. The electric charge between them was unmistakable.

"How is life treating you in West Gidding?" asked Mike as he opened the car door for her..

"Up and down. Maybe it's the result of all the changes. Leaving one country. Going to another. I'm still somewhat disorientated."

"I admire you for your courage."

She flushed, "Life takes many twists."

Mike had a way of penetrating her thinking. He was a lawyer, of course.

"I'm afraid I have to confess that my source of information for the Tate Gallery was wrong. The new exhibition begins next week. We'll only be able to see the usual Turner display."

"What a shame," said Moira.

"But you won't be left without a dose of art. I suggest we go to the Tate first and then visit the Cork Street galleries. I'd also like to know whether you'd like to go to see a Chekhov play that is currently running? It's *The Seagull*, and there's a matinee at 4 pm."

Moira couldn't contain her excitement, "Oh, that would be lovely, thank you!"

“I plan to leave the car at Shoreham, and get the train the rest of the way, as the parking in London is atrocious, especially on a Saturday. Are you happy to traipse around for the whole day?”

“I’d really enjoy that.”

It wasn’t long before they returned to their favourite topic. Moira considered how natural it was for them to talk about painting. They had both completed university studies, then climbed the ladder in their separate careers, and now art brought a passionate interest to both of them in their everyday life.

“I started painting in oils. I loved the smell of them, but they took ages to dry,” said Moira.

“What was your subject matter?”

“Still lifes to start with. For me, there’s something satisfying about defining simple, everyday objects.”

“I find sculpture gives me the same satisfaction, but in 3D. And I also enjoy the texture of oils, when I get the time to use them.”

On arrival at Victoria Station, they set off for

the Tate. Moira hadn't yet seen Turner's paintings in real life, and she and Mike discussed the techniques Turner must have used to create the evocative light. Some of the 4 foot by 6 foot paintings consisted of just sky and sea, or sky and land, fusing together into one whirling vortex of brushstrokes.

"Turner must have used many layers of oils, like Rembrandt did, taking days to dry each time, to achieve this atmospheric effect," said Mike.

They checked out the bookshop, where Mike recommended a thick tome, *The Shock of the New*, which was a current standard text for understanding modern art.

"Now that acrylics and gouache are in vogue, drying time of paint has been reduced to hours," Mike explained, as he tucked his arm through Moira's.

Their next stop took them to the Cork Street Galleries, which Moira had read about, but these specialised in artists who sold well, so the exhibits were more commercial.

Moira hadn't forgotten Mike's long strides on the South Downs, so this time she wore a pair of black patent leather pumps that were elegant but flat-heeled, and allowed her to keep up with his pace. Once the gallery visits were completed, they wandered around London. Instead of taking taxis or the Underground, they opted to tramp around the streets. They dropped in at an agency that sold theatre tickets, and bought some for the afternoon's performance. Mike's knowledge of London was extensive, as he had lived there for several years, so he pointed out buildings of historical interest. Sometimes his factual information was laced with anecdotes, and she enjoyed listening to his tales.

When the drizzle chased them indoors, they went to pubs. Simple fare. Simple conversation. Learning about each other.

"Do you find your day job spills into the weekend?" Moira ventured to ask.

"Sometimes. If I'm working on a complicated case then it does."

"And that cuts into your family time I suppose?"

She saw him raise his eyebrows. Had she gone

too far with her questions? Moira was shocked at her own deviousness.

"Actually no."

A cloud of pain passed over his eyes. Within a second, his eyelids shuttered it out.

"Sorry I didn't mean to pry. I take back my question," said Moira.

"It was your sudden directness which startled me. I've no problem with saying I live on my own." Mike took her hand and caressed her knuckles gently. The sensation rippled through her whole body. When the rain stopped, they continued their strolling, holding hands.

Mid-afternoon, as they sat in comfortable armchairs waiting for the performance to start, sipping the wine Mike had bought, Moira's eyes sparkled at the prospect of attending a theatre performance. She recalled seeing Deborah Kerr, live on stage years ago. She engaged with the hyped-up mood of the crowd spilling into the foyer.

"I always find people-watching fun," she said.

"They're certainly more lively here than at art

exhibitions."

"It's as if the energy of imminent drama has already touched the audience."

Whereas Mike and she had actively engaged in conversation during the day, now they were content to be passive, to be entertained by both arriving audience, and later, actors on stage.

Holding hands, they observed the life of Russian landed gentry. Neither of them knew the play, but the plot was easy to follow, and it lived up to expectations with its acting, provoking lively conversation on the journey home.

On their return to West Gidding, Mike escorted her to the front cottage door, his light caressing kiss brushed her lips, and the sensation left her reeling, then he was gone. The touch of his lips left her longing for more. Once she steadied her hands enough to place the key in the lock, she charged into the cottage. No matter how much they spoke about art, the real reason for the outing had been to spend time together.

Chapter 11

Once again, Moira travelled by train to London on Wednesday. She had collated all her documents into a tidy file and withdrawn some money from the bank the day before. This trip was an expensive necessity, and all the nostalgia she experienced on the previous journey was replaced by an urgency to resolve her visa issues. She had less than six weeks left of her current visa. Today she felt like all the other commuters, a part of the local scene. She was more aware of dirty toilets and litter dropped in the streets.

She had hoped to buy herself a few smart, casual clothes but had to face the reality of cuts in her expenditure. Instead the interview at the Home Office became her main focus. She headed for her appointment with Mary Reid, who studied the original documents she had brought. Then she signed the copies to confirm she had viewed the originals.

"I will retain the signed copies and start the process of obtaining permanent residency. We will notify you when to return to have your passport stamped, probably in three weeks' time as we aren't currently flooded with requests."

"What happens if they don't accept the documents?"

"We'll face that when we come to it. I do know my job, you know. Good luck." A smile cracked the professional exterior, just slightly.

Moira thanked her for everything. The waiting game for the permanent residency would continue for the next few weeks. She would have to be patient.

Zara rang next morning,

"Can we meet up for a coffee today? I have something important I want to discuss."

Moira agreed, but her heart sank. She had hoped to have a quiet day. Zara was already in the deli when Moira arrived. As usual she was brimming with unspent energy and fired away in her direct, almost abrasive, manner.

"I have a work proposal for you."

Moira raised her eyebrows but did not comment.

Scarlett had told her that Zara had almost choked when she mentioned Tony's offer of teaching work for Moira. Zara might be competing with his offer.

"I know you have some knowledge of art, paint yourself and have a variety of work experiences behind you."

"I'm just an amateur painter."

"Every artist starts as an amateur. I need to spend less time in the gallery for personal reasons, so I need an extra pair of hands. She patted her flat, neatly groomed, straight hair. Zara was often abrupt and fidgety, and Moira sensed she would need to be on her guard.

"I don't have my National Insurance number yet. My father sent me some key documents which will allow the Home Office to grant me permanent residency, but it's not been confirmed yet."

Her comment was ignored.

"Now as far as wages go, they are not high. I guess you know there isn't a minimum wage here in the UK at present, but I am prepared to pay you a hundred pounds for a thirty hour week. Your hours will be 10:30 am to 4:30 pm Tuesday to Saturday inclusive. As you take on more responsibilities, I will consider a raise."

Moira was disappointed. The amount sounded paltry compared to her thirty thousand a year salary in Australia, even counting in Australian dollars, but what really mattered to her was living in West Sussex where she was mixing with artists and close to London.

Moira also felt she needed to protect her right to teach Tony's businessmen. It was too lucrative an offer to let go, and besides, she enjoyed the mental stimulus.

"I'm committed to doing some English teaching for Tony for three-day or week-long batches, once every few months."

She felt Zara tense up.

"I thought you would be serious about taking a job at the gallery!"

"I am. But I need the extra money that English teaching will provide me with."

She wasn't prepared to say that Tony paid her

more.

"Can't you teach before and after gallery hours?"

Moira decided to push Zara harder. "I would like to accept your offer but on condition you allow me the freedom to take occasional English classes."

She suspected Zara prized the concept of *freedom* after her escape from Yugoslavia.

"I don't like your suggestion."

"Why don't you give me the job for a trial period?"

Moira persevered. She was not born a negotiator, but life was toughening her up.

"OK. No contract, but you have to start working on Monday. It's going to be an exasperating week with the changeover in exhibitions. You can do the wine and snack ordering." On that note, she said her farewells and left abruptly. Zara must be desperate for help if she caved in so easily. As Moira strolled back to the cottage, she felt her shoulders release the tension from her body. Whether she could work long term with Zara remained to be seen, but at least she had made progress with permanent residency, and would now have a small income which should at least cover her room costs.

Monday saw a curtain of gentle mist hanging over West Gidding. Moira snuggled into bed. This week, her first full week at the gallery, was the countdown to her first exhibition. Tim Copeland, a college lecturer from Sussex University, was showing his oil paintings. They would replace Felicity's water colours which were to be taken down on Wednesday. Hanging Tim's exhibition would take place on Thursday and the opening was scheduled for Friday evening. Zara had already created a press release that had been forwarded to the local media the previous week.

After eating a wholesome English breakfast, Moira marched down to the gallery. As she arrived, the posters for the new exhibition were delivered. She studied them with interest: very modern graphics. She was fortunate not to have had the task of designing them.

Moira tackled the list of jobs Zara had left her.

She rang the deli, ordering cheese, olives and crackers. The off licence shop was the next call. She chatted to the owner who asked,

"The usual order?"

"Yes please. Red and white wines. And the glasses too. Thank you."

She then immersed herself in the task of placing the exhibition invitations in envelopes, and addressing them with the help of Zara's mailing list. They were then divided into two piles: one for posting and one for hand delivery. Zara was adamant about keeping costs down.

She grabbed some business cards, a map that showed the quickest way of walking around the village, and the invitations. A *Back Soon* sign was hung at the door and she took the posters to appropriate venues in the village: the Community Hall, the library, the surgeries and some shops. The rest she posted.

Mid-afternoon, Edward Wishbone arrived. Moira was wary when he greeted her, and she left him free to look at the paintings in all the rooms, undisturbed. She didn't trust him; it wasn't like her to be so suspicious.

"This exhibition ends this week, doesn't it?" he said.

"Yes."

"Felicity has sold well."

"Yes. You'll be receiving an invitation to the opening of the next one on Friday."

"Won't be here."

After that abrupt comment, he sidled out. Moira felt uneasy. She wandered around the exhibition and then saw the space among the mounted drawings that had been displayed on a table. She rang Zara to report the incident. No reply. She left her message.

Zara, Edward Wishbone has just left and a mounted drawing has gone missing.

She worked on later than usual completing one of the dullest jobs: taking picture hooks used for Felicity's paintings out of the walls with pliers, filling the holes, sandpapering them when they were dry, and repainting them with the brilliant white used on the rest of the walls in the gallery.

So, when Scarlett phoned, asking to meet up for coffee, Moira was relieved to end the extended afternoon and join her. After the unpleasant business with Edward, Moira ached to leave the gallery and they set off to a newly opened coffee shop in the next village of Bramber. During the short journey, Moira elaborated on the event of the missing drawing. Her annoyance filtered through her account.

"At least it wasn't a painting," said Scarlett.

"I should have been more careful but who would have thought that Edward, a friend of Zara's, would be the problem? It's so sick."

"Are you sure the drawing was there when you arrived in the morning?"

"Yes."

Scarlett was too loyal a friend for Moira to take her comments personally.

"Well, let Zara sort it out. Accept the experience as part of the tapestry of life. Don't become despondent about it."

"Easier said than done. What about you? What's happening to you?"

"We've been meeting with our lawyers who then argue over the details. Like Nick, I have been looking for somewhere to live. It's difficult giving up home comforts developed over the years. At least we're not arguing over our possessions, as our interests and hobbies have been different in the last six years, so we don't get stuck with arguments about what belongs to whom."

"You have your own cars. What about furniture?"

"Not a problem. I'm prepared to go along with whatever Nick wants, as I feel some sort of need to buy new pieces to celebrate the beginning of a new life."

"That sounds appropriate."

"I'm still going to therapy, but I may have to cut back on that if I want to buy a property. What is new to me is taking charge of my own finances. Nick tended to look after the money side of our life, such as paying bills etc." Scarlett frowned. "You must have experienced those changes yourself. Did you find those difficult?"

"In our marriage, I quickly found out if I didn't take care of the finances, bills, mortgage, etc, they wouldn't be paid. When we were out socially, Guido would be asking me for loans. A very good friend of mine taught me to say no. In later years I found Guido was mesmerised by poker machines. It wasn't a fun flutter; it was a serious addiction." Moira looked uncomfortable. "Much later I was embarrassed to find out he often asked his friends for a *loan,*" her tone emphasised the dubious nature of the transaction, "that was never paid back. Luckily we were leading separate lives by then, and most friends were aware of that. I stopped feeling responsible for his debts."

"It must have been tough."

Next day Zara had already opened the gallery and was waiting for her. Moira checked her watch. She was on time. No problem. Zara started to put coffee in a second cup.

"Let's talk about Edward. What happened?"

"Edward arrived, greeted me, wandered around looking at the paintings, commented that Felicity had done well with her sales, and asked if the exhibition was ending this week. I told him he would be receiving an invitation to the opening on Friday but he said he wouldn't be here. He didn't say goodbye. That's all."

"When did you realise the drawing was missing?"

After he left. I strolled through the exhibition area and saw the gap in the area where the mounted work is displayed. He made no attempt to disguise the space. That's when I rang you."

"Let me think about it. We can't accuse him of theft without evidence. If he comes in again you will have to glue yourself to him. We have always had an open trust policy, and I don't want to install an expensive camera at this stage."

"Can the mounted work be tagged in any way?"

"Too expensive. You'll have to be on your guard more."

"Yes, of course."

Yesterday, Moira had felt upset with Edward for being so deceitful; today she felt disillusioned with Zara's inertia. The gallery would continue to show expensive work, as it wasn't just a provincial gallery, but Zara had a responsibility to protect artists. Moira needed some fresh air to reach her befogged mind, and decided to drop off some extra invitations that Zara had left her.

On the way back to the gallery, Moira popped into the Post Office, and while she was waiting to be served, she overheard the conversation between the postmistress and the owner of the deli. Theft was on the increase. Some items had been removed recently from displays, generally small items. Apparently the Barbour shop was complaining too. The shopkeepers felt they had to coordinate some action. It was hard to imagine that this quiet village had thieves. Even Edward could be classified as such, though her gut feeling was that he had little to do with the general thefts.

On returning to the gallery, Moira repeated the overheard conversation to Zara.

"Would it be possible for all the shopkeepers to join forces and buy security equipment at a discounted price?"

"I will deal with this issue myself? Just let it go."

Moira spent the rest of the day contacting the buyers of Felicity's paintings regarding their pick up. Zara and Moira continued with their set tasks in a prickly silence. Finally Zara said, "I would like you to help with the mounting of the exhibition. When we have an exhibition of mixed artists, it takes longer to arrange the different styles in a cohesive way. As it's one artist this time, we'll get through it all in one day." She sniffed. "You will get the knack of how we work after a couple of times. No?"

Moira doubted that, but she kept her thoughts to herself, and eventually Zara clattered out. The front door opened. The usual tinkling was replaced by a harsher tone due to the increased traffic of painting pick-ups and pre-exhibition preparation. Elizabeth Allthorpe's sister had come to collect Elizabeth's purchase. What a pity she wouldn't be seeing Elizabeth again; she had really liked her. Moira attended to the packing of the painting.

Felicity's entrance was slow, calm and elegant

in comparison. As soon as Moira saw Felicity dressed in a smart jacket and slacks, she realised she herself would be the one loading the paintings into Felicity's car. Felicity's only contribution was to wrap her cherished paintings tenderly in the bubble wrap she had brought with her, as if she had all day to complete her task. Moira's patience was ebbing, but she knew better than to speak out. After an hour and a half, Felicity left. Moira's shoulders and back ached, and she longed for a hot shower. She locked up the gallery and staggered home.

Chapter 12

On Thursday morning when Moira woke up, her body felt as if it had been through a wringer. The windows were rattling as if they had a message to relay to her. Had she left them open? She only remembered arriving home, her ablutions and going to bed. She parted the curtains and looked out of the window. The crying sky competed with the gale. Rain drummed on the roof, and flattened the early pansies Pat had planted in the front garden. The flowerpots were brimming over with excess water, and the wind had blown off roof slates which now lay on the pavement in pieces. Several broken-off tree branches were gyrating down the main street and some waste paper was swirling violently. How had she not heard the howling during the night? She had no appetite for a walk against the full force of the gale, let alone for unloading large oil paintings and carrying them into the gallery.

She made herself a strong coffee and returned to bed for five more minutes. The warmth of her bed tempted her to stay at home for longer, but tasks left over from Wednesday awaited her. Reluctantly she headed for the bathroom.

As she trudged to the gallery, the almost-horizontal rain slapped her face. The ferocious wind stung her skin, her clothes billowed out and her shoes squished with too much water. When Tim arrived with his van-load of paintings, the gale had increased in intensity, and one painting was whipped out of his hands, crashing on to the pavement. Moira pulled her Barbour jacket on and went out to help. Even with the two of them handling the large canvases, it was a strenuous battle against the elements, that threatened her with a possible fall. She gritted her teeth – oh for her life in Sydney.

When Zara stumbled in shortly afterwards, she began arranging the paintings on the wooden floor. She made no mention of the missing drawing. Every so often she stood back to assess the visual effect, and asked Moira to adjust the position of individual paintings to her satisfaction. Only then did the hanging of paintings take place.

Moira typed up labels with the painting title, the artist's name and the price. They would be blue-tacked to the wall beside each painting, the next day. Again, it was well after closing time by the time they were finished. She felt a tight knot in her chest, as she typed up the list of paintings which would be distributed to viewers.

In the evening, she took a sleeping tablet to relax her. The next day would be demanding.

Friday brought more wind, prowling in search of victims to sweep along the street. Like a robot, Moira hung the typed labels beside the paintings, distributed the leaflets about Tim round the gallery and set out the glasses and wine that the off-licence had delivered.

She returned to the gallery at 6 pm. Zara, in a startling black and red creation, was poised to welcome those who had battled the elements to attend Tim's exhibition preview. An American lady was the first to arrive. She introduced herself as living at the Mayfair Hotel in London, but was visiting West Gidding for a few days for some bridge competition.

A glass of wine in hand, she admired the paintings, but insisted on espousing her philosophy of life to Moira, and anyone else who would listen to her. Her monologue referred to disappointments in life. That's all Moira needed.

"We are the ones who disappoint ourselves and hence avoid happiness," she said. "We do this by having too high expectations for ourselves. Usually unachievable ones."

Moira smiled and nodded but removed herself from the lady to welcome new arrivals. Slowly the number of people in the gallery grew; it appeared that all the great in the county had turned up, despite the weather. Luckily the front door where the wines were being served had been left open to allow fresh air to enter. People jostled for space at the same time as balancing their glasses of wine. Since the tables of food couldn't be reached easily, Moira served savouries on a platter, edging her way through the now-lively crowd. Wine was loosening people's inhibitions. She noted Charles had arrived without Felicity, and introduced him to Scarlett who was also on her own. When she passed them again they were engrossed in animated conversation, huddled together, Scarlett's flirtatious eyes sparkling. Four paintings proudly sported red spots; a positive sign.

The exhibition opening was in full swing when Edward Wishbone arrived, helping himself to a glass of wine at the entrance. Moira noticed him swaying from side to side. He then plodded towards the corner of the room, bumping into the milling guests on the way. What was he up to? Then she noticed his shaking hands as he tried to strike a match to light his cigarette. In this fire-prone building. Was he crazy? She tried to squeeze between people to reach him but she was too late.

His fumbling hands had dropped the match near a fistful of leaflets on a small table. The flickering sparks had quickly ignited the paper, which soon began to hiss and crackle as the fire took hold. Zara screamed for people to evacuate. A coil of smoke curled up towards the ceiling, and the acrid smoke burnt Moira's throat. Tim grabbed the fire extinguisher, but was blocked from the fire by people panicking and shrieking, as they tried to push their way out. Scarlett rang the fire brigade.

In the meantime, the sea of flames became a horrific devouring monster. Some of the flames leaped towards the ceiling, scorching it. As the gallery emptied out, Tim was able to direct the extinguisher at the growing blaze. Oh no, the paintings! Pressing wet cloths to her mouth, Moira grabbed the paintings nearest the fire and placed them in the recessed porch.

Against the background of heat and activity, Edward stood nonplussed, almost defying the flames, and yet spellbound by them. Moira's fury at his drunken behaviour galvanised her into action, jerking him roughly out of the gallery. When the cold rain outside contacted her face, she blinked, as if waking up to her aggressive act.

It was a small village so the fire brigade arrived within minutes. This helped to speed up further evacuation as well as extinguish the fire. The shrieks and groans continued as the crowd surged outside, and the raindrops brought relief as they spattered the blackened faces among the onlookers. The police parked their car in front of the building and cordoned off the area.

By this time Zara had moved the oil paintings from inside to outside the front door of the gallery. They would be safe under the awning, despite the persistent drizzle that had replaced the previous downpour.

Once the fire was extinguished, the extent of the damage was visible. The majority was in one corner in the back of the front room, where black soot covered the walls and ceiling. It had helped that the walls of the gallery had absorbed the moisture from the recent heavy rains. Elsewhere the smoke had coated the interior of the gallery with a film of dark grey opaqueness. A folder of mounted artists' work and printed leaflets had been damaged. Despite the turmoil and panic, Tim felt upbeat because his paintings had been saved.

Zara looked haggard and distressed; no doubt she was thinking about costs of damage and insurance. They were all questioned by the police, who were collating information for a report. This officialdom benumbed Moira, but when questioned, she felt obliged to mention Edward's attempts to light a cigarette.

"Was there any evidence of Edward Wishbone drinking?" the policeman asked.

She looked at Zara.

"Yes."

Moira explained her actions had been delayed by the density of the crowd between herself and Edward.

Everything seemed so dreamlike. It was midnight by the time broken glass had been swept up to avoid accidents, and edible food removed and stored. Moira felt like collapsing in a heap. Nobody spoke. Moira stacked all the glasses by the sink but said she would return next morning to wash them. The last twenty-four hours had seen her drenched several times and she felt the symptoms of a cold.

After the evening's turmoil, Moira lay in bed gazing into the darkness of her future. What would happen now? It was as if the tension and the challenges since her arrival in West Sussex had forced open a dam. She submitted to the fury of her emotions, as heartfelt sobs tore her body with gut-wrenching force. Unrelenting home-sickness gnawed at her heart, and she wept until her body had spent all its energies, leaving her limp and drained. Oblivion was easier than facing reality, and finally she fell asleep, where nothing could reach her, where there was no love, no pain, no hope.

When Moira woke up, the recesses of her mind were blank. Her head throbbed, her gritty eyes burned and her throat was swollen. She was thirsty. She felt as if the Universe had spat her out. Damn Edward's stupidity. He was a reprehensible man. What a waste of time and energy. Would Zara continue with her gallery? Was she without a job? She rolled over and tried to sleep.

She sank into a dream. She was lying on a never ending stretch of beach. The white sand was clinging to her body sticky from sun lotion. The sky's gentle blue hung over the beach. The sun was in its early morning gentle heat and enveloped the sea and sand. Paradise. Time was suspended in that moment of tranquillity. No future. No past.

The smell of ground coffee beans began to tease her nostrils. She heard a knock and a latch lifting in the distance. She opened her eyes. Pat had switched on the light in her room and was carrying a tray with eggs and bacon, coffee and hot toast. Slowly Moira raised her aching body to accept this unlooked for gesture of kindness.

"I thought you might need this to start the day," said Pat. "Do you have any side effects from the smoke?"

Moira stared at a collection of puckered blisters she'd just noticed on her hand. "Just these."

"They look angry. I'll leave out some soothing cream for you downstairs."

Moira squinted at her watch. "I've slept in. I better turn up at the gallery."

"I wouldn't be in a rush. Zara won't be able to do much until the insurance inspector has been and written a report. Enjoy your breakfast in bed."

"Thank you so much."

The luxury of breakfast in bed was welcome. When she opened the curtains, she saw the sky looking overcast but settled, now that the storm had passed. She lingered in her room in her out-of-body state, tidying the crumpled, smoke-filled clothes. Her throat still burned. Shaken, her anger was directed at Edward. She mustered enough energy to take a shower and get dressed, and steeled herself for the day.

When she reached the gallery, a sign announcing it to be *TEMPORARILY CLOSED* had been pasted across the glass of the front window. The inside of the gallery smelt of smoke and humidity. Pale faced, Zara stood amidst the chaos, her shoulders drooped, her face betraying exhaustion and resignation. When she emerged from her daydream and noticed Moira, she came to life.

"I suppose you had to blab that Edward was the cause of the fire."

"Like you, I was questioned by the police and the fire brigade."

"Did you have to be so explicit about Edward?"

"What is it with you? He was the sole cause of the fire... AND he was so drunk he was unable to walk." She shook her head in disgust. "He was swaying from side to side as he stumbled in."

"So why didn't you stop his smoking?" shrieked Zara.

"I tried but everyone was sardined in the gallery. I didn't reach him in time," responded Moira with equal force. "He's your friend. He should have known better."

Moira felt she had probably crossed some unacceptable invisible line but her impatience with Edward's carelessness had not disappeared. And why did Zara always defend him?

"I better start on the dishes."

She wheeled around abruptly and marched out to the back room. If Zara aggravated her with more comments, she would lose her cool. When finished, Moira phoned the off-licence to say the glasses were ready for a pick-up.

Moira found that the cold symptoms from the previous day were now developing into fully fledged flu, with aches and pains. The rawness of her throat was intense, and it wasn't just the result of smoke. She stocked up on paracetamol and cough mixture at the pharmacy and slunk back to bed. She slept for the next twenty-four hours.

On Sunday, Scarlett arrived armed with best-sellers, lemons and honey to comfort her. Ensconced in bed for most of the day, Moira sniffed her way through dozens of tissues, consumed gallons of water spiked with lemons and ginger, and enjoyed the cosiness of her duvet. She alternated between naps and reading. Pat relayed the rumour that was spreading: Edward had been Zara's lover years ago and was jealous of her success as a gallery owner. By the afternoon, her temperature had gone down and she felt hungry enough to eat. Tony had rung and suggested taking her to the pub for a meal, promising to bring her back straight away. Ironically, her illness had brought her friends closer to her.

In the evening, Zara phoned to announce that the gallery would be closed for a week because the insurance inspectors were to coming to inspect the damage, but she didn't know exactly when. The half-burnt remains of the interior needed to be removed. She was anxious to keep business moving after the fire, despite some minor construction work and painting, so she asked Moira to work the following week, mornings-only, to answer telephone calls, check the mail and allow visitors to view a revamped version of the exhibition in the back rooms. Her salary would, of course, be reduced.

Having encountered seismic upheavals in recent months, Moira longed to lose herself in some sketching and painting. Life had mainly revolved around everyday survival issues, and excluded the passion which had brought her to the UK in the first place. As the gallery work had been interrupted, she could devote herself to art now. She dug into the wardrobe for her drawing materials and headed off to a part of the village which was new to her.

It was there that she came across a church which had a Norman tower. The textures changed at one end of the stone building and she concluded an extra wing had been added at a later date. She strolled through the hushed ranks of gravestones in the churchyard, and peered at the headstones covered with leafy lichens. She tried to decipher the inscriptions, and found a few going back to the seventeenth century. She shivered, though it was a warm day, and she could smell freshly cut grass from nearby cottage gardens. The bells struck up a carillon, shattering the silence.

Drawing small sketches, she positioned herself in different places; on the grass, on the bank edging the graveyard. Finally, she sat down on the stone wall and applied herself to a vertical view that appealed to her. She was absorbed in setting out the angles of the upper part of the church, when a car pulled up near the wall, and a man called out, “I hope I can have a copy of that.”

The interruption irritated Moira as it made her lose her concentration and momentum. When she turned round, she noticed the clerical collar around the man’s neck.

"I don't know if my standard of drawing will be good enough for you. By the way I'm Moira Capaldi."

"I realised you were a new face in the village."

"I was here on holiday in January but have returned for good, I hope."

"Welcome to West Gidding then." he said, unlocking the side door to the church with a six inch metal key, and disappearing inside.

She became of aware of the temperature dropping, so sauntered to the back of the church, where bluebells were fighting their way through the weeds below a large oak tree. She loved the vibrant blue of the flowers; they reminded her of Mike's eyes. From this angle she could include the flowers and some of the lower branches of the oak tree as a foreground for the drawing. Later, she would transfer all this preliminary preparation on to canvas and then work it into an oil painting. She resolved to return several times later in the week. She packed up her materials and headed for the cottage.

The hedges were filled with mallow, and

bunches of heavy cream blossoms festooned the hawthorn trees. As always, she felt refreshed and calmed by her contact with nature. As she swung into a steady rhythm of walking, she pondered. Teaching bonded her with Tony, art was what connected her to Mike. Light humour underlay the fabric of Tony's life. Mike on the other hand had a seriousness and an intensity about him that may have been caused by some tragedy, or maybe it was just his personality. It gave him sensitivity in keeping with his interest in art. She developed Tony's teaching ideas and Mike extended her horizons in art. She fully enjoyed the company of both men. An intriguing triangle.

Four days later Zara was on the phone again. Her tone of voice had acquired a mellowness, and was tinged with excitement.

"We have to meet up at the deli. I have something special to show you."

Moira was settled in her seat when Zara rushed into the deli clutching a large envelope in her hand. Carefully she unwrapped the delicate papers inside.

“Look Moira. Look what I found!”

She revealed a bundle of letters on cream paper tied with a blue ribbon. When Zara took them out, the powdery sheets of thin notepaper appeared ragged at the edges.

“The insurance inspector was poking around in the area between the gallery ceiling and the upstairs room when he found a locked metal box with this bundle of letters inside.”

Moira observed more closely. The fragile pages were loose and she handled them with care. Zara was pulling out some of the ones she had read. “Just look at these pages. They are letters written by Lady Penfold and sent to her lover, Lewis.”

“She must have been taught to read and write,” said Moira. “I suppose Lewis must have lived in the building that is now your gallery, if they were found there.”

“Had they been made public in her day, they would have created a greater scandal.”

They continued to examine the letters. “Do they have dates on them or at least the year?” said Moira.

"Can't make out the date. Maybe 1890."

Moira peered more closely.

"There's something here about the Penfold family. Some of them emigrated to South Australia."

"What a coincidence," said Moira. "There's a Penfold brand of wine. I wonder if the two are connected. South Australia was populated solely by free settlers, so there was more personal freedom to start businesses."

Zara started to put the loose papers back into the envelope.

"What shall we do with them?" said Moira. "They're not easy to decipher. Perhaps they should be handed over to the Historical Society."

"We'll talk about it later. I always felt there were dark energies in the gallery. I have to go now." She gathered her belongings and said, "By the way, are you free tomorrow night? Felicity Green asked if you would like to go with me to dinner at their home."

Sharing the discovery of the letters seemed to have softened Zara, or maybe it was the disastrous fire which had left her vulnerable.

"Yes. I'll be happy to come."

Chapter 13

Moira went downstairs a few minutes before Zara was due to arrive. She heard the knock on the wooden front door. She smiled; at least it wasn't a doorbell. The stunning dress Zara wore was designed to have black panels overlapping yellow ochre panels. They looked so classy, and definitely not from the mediocre range of a department store.

"Zara where do you get your designer clothes from?"

"I have the design in my head," She touched her forehead theatrically. "Then I draw it on paper. Sometimes I paint it." She flung her right arm into a painting position.

"I have a very good dressmaker, a Russian. She and I understand each other well." Her tone changed to a quietly confidential one. "She gets samples of material and suggests further amendments to my design. Her advice is based on the practicalities of sewing. So you see we combine our skills very well."

"Would there be any chance of her making

something for me?"

"You would have to speak to her. Maybe if she likes you, she will find the time."

Zara was driving Moira into the heartland of village life in West Sussex. The pre-dusk light emphasized the maturity of the trees that made Sussex special; oaks, beeches and birches, all with their distinctive shapes. The trees were clothed with the first spring foliage, a piercing apple green, which summer would change into darker variations, depending on the tree. The sky was a pale, cornflower blue. The sun stretched its peach tentacles to invade the blue. As if allowing feelings to filter through her thoughts Zara said, "I love this countryside. You know it reminds me of Yugoslavia where I come from. I feel at peace in this landscape."

Moira waited for her to say more, wanted to ask about her experiences, but said nothing. It was the first time Zara had spoken about herself, and Moira didn't want to break into Zara's thoughts, but she'd already clammed up.

Moira turned her thoughts to the landscape they

were passing through. She mused how different the sunburnt land of Australia was. Ninety-five per cent of the population lived in cities. It was a society dependent on cars so walking was not fashionable. She had been happy with her lifestyle in Sydney but it dawned on her that her heart had always been attracted to the cultural life of Europe.

"By the way Moira, I have a suggestion for you. Actually it came from the vicar. How would you like to teach some art classes to children up to the age of twelve? Saturday mornings. About an hour. A pound per person. What you could do is work towards a children's art exhibition. Then you could invite the parents and make publicity for the next classes," said Zara, always the business woman.

It seemed as if it was a *fait accompli* and she was expected to start the classes straightaway. Moira was concerned about losing her freedom on Saturdays, without the security of a permanent job. "I suppose I could use the back room as it hasn't seen much damage."

"You have to be comfortable with doing the

classes *and* keeping an eye on the gallery."

So this was Zara's plan. Now that she had started, Zara barrelled along. "Always charge for the term in advance. A missed lesson is a missed lesson. Children get sick, go away with their parents unexpectedly. We can't be messing with catching upon missed lessons."

"We could start at ten. The kids would be fresher then, and if we had the numbers, a second class could begin at half past eleven."

"Begin the classes as soon as you are ready. I want the gallery functioning while it's being revamped."

They had reached the outlying part of Hayward's Heath and were turning into a driveway. She saw a stately, moderately-sized house surrounded by a manicured garden. Zara pulled up in the parking area, and they emerged from the car. The front door opened and Charles Green greeted them both warmly. He appeared relaxed and was casually dressed in beige linen slacks and a cream open-necked shirt. He announced one guest had dropped out because of sickness, but no matter they would still have their fun. This suited Moira, as she preferred to get to know people beyond a superficial level, and this was only possible in an intimate group.

Zara reintroduced her to the elegant and refined Felicity, the epitome of establishment in Sussex. Definitely County. Moira had brought flowers, rather than the bottle of wine that would have been customary in Sydney. Somehow it seemed more suited to the formality of the occasion. They were shepherded from the entry hall into the reception area on the left. She glanced over to where a previous arrival was sitting and her jaw dropped. Her rude visitor from the gallery was ensconced in one of the comfortable armchairs, his legs stretched in front of him. He at least had the grace to rise and greet her as he was introduced as the artist Edward Wishbone. Nodding his head, he mumbled, “Good evening,” somewhat indistinctly.

It seemed he was going to play by the social rules in front of Felicity. Moira noticed that Edward’s pot belly was more noticeable, now that he wasn’t wearing his long coat. After a pre-dinner sherry, the group moved to the dining room on the right where the crystal glasses glinted on the table, reflecting the light of the candelabras. The damask napkins lay beside the polished Victorian silver cutlery. The lively seating process contrasted with the cool elegance of setting and dress. The chatter exuded a familiarity only possible between close friends.

As the newcomer to the group, Moira found she was listening more than contributing to the conversation, her eyes taking in the nineteenth century antiques at the same time. Gossip seemed to be on the agenda at this dinner party. It appeared that the greater the notoriety of the scandal, the more it brought an artist fame and prominence. Felicity and Edward seemed to compete for attention by talking about their forthcoming art exhibitions, as if needing to draw attention to themselves. Zara occasionally acted as referee and aired her knowledge about the latest exhibitions on show in London.

Moira had assumed that Zara had brought her here to meet artists as part of her gallery work and had been expecting the artists to discuss the latest developments in the art world. By the time the present company were prepared to talk about provocative art in London, Moira had sensed a tension between Zara and Edward.

Moira was picking up clues about the social structure of West Sussex society. Zara seemed beyond any English class system, so probably moved in and out of social classes to suit her commercial purposes. Her stylish mode of dressing was in keeping with her role as art gallery owner, and perhaps her custom-designed clothes made her acceptable to all classes.

Charles seemed to be allotted the task of pouring the two French wines on offer, Chablis or Châteauneuf-du-Pape, while the maid served the dinner. This consisted of a classic entree of Scottish smoked salmon with lemon, followed by roast venison with all the traditional vegetables: roast potatoes and parsnips, carrots and beans. Cheese and biscuits as well as chocolate mousse graced the table next.

When Charles dropped down on to the chair beside her, Moira asked him what work he did. She had opened her mouth before thinking. It wasn't very English to be so open. He admitted to being a high school teacher, which surprised her, but then Felicity's family was wealthy stock. Oil painting was his love. He confessed that he and Felicity had no children, which confirmed what Scarlett had told her. Apparently Felicity was dedicated to her painting and did not want to be another Barbara Hepworth.

"What do you mean?" Moira frowned. She felt she was missing some important piece of information.

"Barbara Hepworth was a talented sculptor in West Cornwall at a time when sculpture was dominated by men." Charles helped himself to some more cheese. "In fact she was the only woman sculptor in her time and lived in St Ives with Ben Nicholson. They had triplets. After three years, the children were booked into a home where they could be cared for because Barbara was so focussed on her career. She would visit them there, and they would be booked in to see her at her studio. Naturally, society regarded what she did as scandalous."

"So you're saying that Felicity felt having children would detract from her artistic life, or at least create a conflict between her art and her parenting?" Moira said.

"Exactly," replied Charles.

She liked his quiet, down to earth manner, and found talking to him was easier than talking to Felicity and Edward, who seemed so preoccupied with society and appearances. Moira couldn't help feeling that Felicity and Charles seemed an ill-matched couple.

Moira raised her eyebrows when Zara excused them from staying for coffee and liqueurs. Once they were in the car, and Zara was adjusting her driving gloves, Moira said, "I have to tell you, Edward was downright rude to come tonight. After all the fire business."

"Are you upset he ignored you tonight?" Zara shot back.

She started to fidget with her hands on the wheel.

"The issue isn't whether I was ignored tonight or not. The issue is what is acceptable behaviour from eccentric artists." Moira was aware she was pushing Zara's buttons but was too tired to care.

"Stop. That's enough."

Zara's tone was cold. The drive back to West Gidding seemed shorter, or maybe their senses were dulled by wine or disagreement. After Moira got out of the car, Zara put her foot down on the accelerator with gusto, and shot off into the night.

In the first week of the gallery's reopening, Moira arrived to find that Zara had left her the ledger books to study. Moira sat down at the reception table. The best way of attacking the subject was to peruse what had been recorded previously. Maths had not been her best subject at school but there was always the calculator to help her. She turned her attention to the May entries. The income and expenditure were entered under two separate headings. That was straightforward. The expenditure corresponded to the entries in the receipt book or petty cash withdrawals.

The receipts would have to be sorted out in a chronological sequence before she started writing up the entries for expenditure, to avoid erasing entries. It was going to be a painstakingly boring and irritating process. She wished she hadn't offered to learn about book-keeping. It was typical that when she welcomed distractions, few people visited the gallery. The doorbell would have at least woken her up. Just then the ringing of the phone shattered her concentration.

"Good morning, West Gidding Gallery," she said.

No reply. Probably a wrong number.

The gallery in its burnt state was giving her claustrophobia. Moira started formulating the content of the children's lessons due to start soon. Perhaps a famous painting could be chosen for class discussion, something containing human figures, she mused. Her guided questions would elicit the story behind the painting: the youngsters would be asked to describe the clothes of the people in the painting, what were they saying and feeling. The personality of the children in front of her would determine what ideas emerged. Then she would play some appropriate music and ask the children to paint a modern version of the painting...

The phone rang again. No reply. Just another interruption to her lesson planning. Reluctantly putting aside her work, she reported the malfunction of the phone to British Telecom.

It was a pity she didn't already have some children's paintings to superimpose on the poster. So she would have to use bright colours in the lettering.

Have fun with your painting!

Come to classes at your own West Gidding Gallery

Saturdays at 10 am

There was a short phone call from Mike to say he had been called away on business to London and would be away for a few days. He claimed he would miss her and she warmed to his words, glad they were continuing to see each other. So the phone was working...

She was about to lock up the gallery when the

BT engineers rang to say they had checked out the gallery phone and it was functioning perfectly. When the phone rang again the same evening, with no caller audible, at number 36 she deduced she must be the target of nuisance calls. She rang BT again, and they suggested that if there were more such calls, she should have them intercepted. She couldn't see that as a solution as she didn't own the line herself. It wouldn't be fair to Pat or Zara. A tricky and disquieting situation; maybe she could buy a whistle to blow the ears off the nuisance caller.

In the next few days Moira had more to contend with. Zara charged in, as if on a mission.

"I'd like to talk to you about going to France with me," she said.

"A trip to France? Oh. I can't afford it at present."

"No need for you to worry about that. We'll aim to be away for only five days. We'll make the crossing by ferry from Newhaven to Dieppe. We can head for Honfleur and then roam around, or stay put."

"What documents do I need for France? Do I

need a visa for an Australian passport?"

"You must stop living in fear about visas. You have to be positive about these issues, trust me."

Moira bit her lip. She must stop being so twitchy about her travel documents, but of course, Tony could also help her if she needed a visa.

Her head was humming with ideas for the trip. If they travelled in Zara's car, she could pay her share of the petrol, and the ferry of course. She sensed that Zara would be careful with money, so meals would be modest in price. Her past experience of French food was that its quality, freshness and variety were unsurpassed. So accommodation was the only costly item.

Moira returned to the cottage. Pat was away. Preparing an omelette for herself, she thought of her last trip to France, when she had been passionate about her history of art course. Seeing paintings in European galleries was an improvement on studying them in books. The scale was what made a difference to the appreciation of composition, colour and tone. In Paris, the Pompidou Centre and the Picasso

Museum had impressed her.

Slowly she came back from her reverie, and her practical common sense kicked in. Was it wise to travel with such a strong personality as Zara?

Mike had returned to West Gidding, reminding Moira that his invitation to his studio was still open. She was astonished at his willingness to show his studio and share his ideas about art, as most artists possessively guarded their artistic space. He was keen to explain his method of working with abstraction. She had an insatiable curiosity to discover how he achieved this.

They met for a ploughman's lunch at *The George*, and she felt hot under his scrutiny.

"You have some crumbs on your upper lip," he said, gently wiping them off with a napkin while she flushed as he leaned towards her.

She was relieved to leave the pub and avoid the intensity of his gaze. He drove her to his elegant semi, where a large room was designated for his artwork. She busied herself checking out his studio. He had huge canvases stacked on the floor at one end of the room. Jars, tubes and brushes were stacked according to variety of paint along one shelf; four areas, one each for acrylic, gouache, water colours and oils. Turps and linseed oil were stored on another shelf. Moira was struck by the tidiness of it all. She dropped to a wooden seat beside a trestle table.

"I love the posters you have hung on the walls. Are they of London art exhibitions?"

"Yes, I had a phase when I would buy one at each exhibition I attended. Colourful aren't they?"

"Indeed. So, show me how you create abstraction."

Mike pulled out a folder of his charcoal sketches of a springtime wood, which were realistically drawn, almost photographically. Then he showed off the versions painted in quick-drying acrylics, representational again except for the colours; he had used blues, reds and yellows in many different combinations. His observation and painting skills were undeniable.

"So, how did all this work for you when you

painted?"

"Let me show you."

He pulled out some large canvases in oils, a smile playing about his lips. The simplified group of trees had now become three simple trunk shapes in the next canvas. The last canvas showed three vertical stripes of colour: pink, emerald green and navy. Had he shown her the last painting first she wouldn't have known that the three stripes were derived from trees. In a few minutes, he had succeeded in showing her the entire abstracting process where form was simplified to the barest essentials.

She was amazed at the structural simplicity of the process. It made her appreciate Picasso's work. After all his representational painting was equal to Rembrandt's or Michelangelo's, when he was sixteen, so to progress as a painter, he had been compelled to introduce innovation.

"Enough of all this theory."

Mike took her hand and led her to the lounge where she seated herself on the cream leather sofa. He brought out a platter of smoked salmon and dishes of olives and cheeses.

"Would you like a glass of Bollinger Champagne?" said Mike.

His fingers brushed against her hand as he reached for the glasses on the side table. The movement created a tingle that spread to the extremities of her body. She edged away from him disguising it as a readjustment of her seating. It was the first time she had felt desire in a long time.

He seated himself on the sofa beside her, and so began a long conversation where Moira directed questions at him about galleries and artistic trends in London. She felt flustered by his almost-gaping admiration.

At the cottage, she regurgitated the afternoon's scenario. She had appreciated that Mike's approach to painting was cerebral or intellectual, probably because he was a lawyer. The Impressionism, which she was drawn to, seemed to be an expression of emotions through colour. Grateful to Mike for sharing his ideas, she would now experiment with his method in her own time. Perhaps even marry the two approaches, combine the intellectual with the emotional. Alongside the common interest in art, there was always the silent electric current of attraction that passed between them.

It was a month since Moira had left him. Guido had visited Moira's solicitor to discuss legal matters. In a fit of persuasiveness, he had tried to coax an address from Moira's parents and friends, but no information had been leaked to him. He now knew about her return to the UK, which left him feeling more desolate than he would have expected. Yes, he missed the salmon mousse, Filipino chicken and the Hungarian torte she made, but it was more than that. Intimacy was more important than sex in a long term relationship. He still couldn't grasp why she had erased her life with him to put squiggles on paper or canvas. How could she replace their materially comfortable life in Sydney for an artist's life? She was crackers.

Chapter 14

Next day, Moira had her posters ready for the children's classes at the gallery. Her first call was to the library. "I'm Moira Capaldi from West Gidding Gallery," she said as she handed over her poster.

"Hello. I'm Katy Bryant."

Moira asked whether children in the village would be interested in painting classes at the gallery.

"My two would love to come."

"I'm planning to have one hour long lessons, on Saturdays at 10 am. Probably for five weeks."

"Super."

"Might they have some friends who would like to come too?"

"Mmm, yes, I expect so. Have you got any brochures for the classes? I'll hand them around the other mums."

"I only have the posters, but I will come back with brochures later this week. The other thing they may find fun is that their work will be exhibited, probably at the end of the five weeks."

"I'll spread the news."

"Thank you so much."

And Moira continued her poster drop-offs at the Historical Society, pubs and schools. Uneasy, her thoughts kept returning to Zara's suggestion of going to France. Working with Zara was one thing, but spending five days travelling with her didn't feel right. She herself was drained of energy and had no stomach for extensive travel by car. Oh my… it felt as if Zara was beginning to create a stranglehold over her personal life, the little she had at present. She suspected Zara would feel affronted by her refusal, and there would be a confrontation as a result, but she would have to be firm in saying no.

As Tony's businessmen continued to arrive steadily during the summer, Moira and Tony fell into a comfortable pattern of co-existing professionally at the school during the day and interacting socially at the end of the day in the pub. They had switched to *The George,* a quieter pub, which hung on to a faded grandeur belonging to the past. Tony took great delight in introducing her to typically English dishes such as *bangers and mash* and *toad in the hole.* Moira enjoyed the fluidity with which they connected when they shared their teaching past and travel experiences: Tony had spent twelve months in Australia and Asia liked to talk about his adventures. He had really taken to the open egalitarian society in Australia, so different from the structured class system of West Sussex. In return, Moira related some of her air hostessing highlights, such as sharing a car with the crew to visit the Shah's ski lodge in Tehran. They competed for laughter with their stories, and Moira allowed herself to ponder on what it might be like to travel with Tony.

One Wednesday evening, Tony and Moira were having their usual after-work drink when Tony announced he was going to the *Duke of York*, an alternative cinema in Brighton for a showing of an Ingmar Bergman film called *Fanny and Alexander*. Would she like to go with him? They felt like a couple of kids spilling out of school. They reached Brighton early enough to try out a Thai meal, not far from the cinema.

The film, which depicted a family saga, took them from tears of laughter to joy to sadness. They had plenty to chat about as Tony drove them back to West Gidding.

"By the way, I have been given two tickets for a concert at the Festival Hall next week. Fancy going?"

"Oh, any idea of what's in the programme?"

"The Schumann piano concerto."

"A favourite of mine. I didn't know you liked classical music."

"Yes, but I don't often get the chance to get away from the school."

"OK, yes, thank you, I'd love to go."

It wasn't till she was home in the evening that she recognized it had been a sort of date. She liked the way their fun was interspersed with seriousness, and yet there were no romantic vibes for her in that relationship, nothing compared to the heady giddiness she experienced with Mike.

Back at school next day, Tony asked how her Chinese students coped with the English exams in their literature subject. Feeling her hackles rise ever so slightly, she wondered why she was so irritated with his questions about the Chinese students.

"They had to have a pass in English, which involved reading six novels, studying poetry and several plays all telescoped into one year, unlike the Australian students who took two years to do the same. They were prepared to spend eight hours on homework if that's what it took to reach their goals. They were very bright but they had to be taught essay writing as a skill."

"How did you do that?"

"We would analyse typical examination questions and then I would teach them how to divide the question into three or four segments, that would provide them with the paragraphs for their essays. They had to learn that in English thinking, the main point appeared in the first sentence of a paragraph. Just a different way of thinking to theirs."

"I never thought of language that way."

Recently someone had told her that Tony's father had been captured by the Japanese during

World War II, but that was the Japanese not the Chinese. Not everybody had her ability to scrutinize a face and identify it as Chinese or Japanese.

When Moira woke up next morning, her nightshirt was soaking wet with perspiration and she was disorientated. She tried to remember her dream. It was the time of the French Revolution, her husband had disappeared during one of the mob attacks on the Bastille and she was left alone with six children to feed, including the youngest, a babe of two months. She had no milk in her breasts for the little one, and his wail of hunger was a grating one. The stench of dead bodies abandoned in the street made her feel nauseated.

Now fully awake, Moira tried to brush aside the disturbing images, but the feeling of helplessness persisted. Why did she have this dream? Was it a past life experience? If so what was the relevance to her present life? Did it have something to do with this room? She thought of the hand incident; maybe there was a connection between the dream and Lady

Penfold haunting this room? Enough of that!

Next day, she was returning from the shops when an older lady caught hold of her sleeve, saying, "Cross my hand with money."

Though wearing a white peasant blouse and a long, red and white patterned skirt, she seemed to reflect the greyness of the sky. Large loop earrings adorned her ears, and jewellery jingled along her slim arms, but her eyes were fired up with energy and light. Moira felt hypnotized by her, but didn't want to engage with fantasy and strode off. The woman followed her and said, "Two men are in love with you at present."

Moira stopped in her tracks.

"Cross my hand with two pounds."

Moira slipped her hand into her handbag, struggled to find the coins, and placed them in the woman's suntanned hands.

"The cottage had to be exorcised…"

The old woman had probably heard the gossip about the fire. Moira regretted she had weakened in her resolve to walk away.

"What do you mean, exorcised?" Moira queried, with a tone of resignation.

"You have to work it out yourself. Just remember the history of Lady Penfold," and she whirled round and disappeared into the crowds at a nearby fête.

The surprise encounter renewed Moira's sense of disorientation. It was so unbelievable. Her cautious, logical thinking wanted to reject such happenings, but then she recalled how she had felt the coldness in the bedroom during her room inspection of number 36. Then there was the hand incident. Could all this be connected with Lady Penfold? Impossible.

However, the incident encouraged her to do more research on West Gidding history. It turned out that Sussex had a brutish, pagan past. It was the last county to be converted to Christianity, and was known for its unsavoury element until the sixteenth century. Escaped criminals, highwaymen and undesirables frequented its lanes, but all that changed when Brighton became a spa town in the eighteenth century. These days, West Sussex was rich, Christian and respectable, but it seemed that the old energies still lurked behind the outwardly civilised appearances.

The village of West Gidding had seen violence in Lord Penfold's day. His actions to remove his wife's lover were testament to the fact that the man was below their station in society and therefore a slur on Lord Penfold's name; not dissimilar to the class conflict between Connie Reid, a cultured upper-class bohemian and Oliver Mellors, a gamekeeper in D. H. Lawrence's, *Lady Chatterley's Lover.*

Moira was glad she had accepted the invitation to the concert in London. It suited her that Tony was laid back and liked casual clothes. He didn't create problems for himself with rigid expectations or perfectionism. They stopped at a restaurant in Henfield for an early supper. Asian fare this time – Yum Prawn soup followed by Thai Red Curry chicken, all accompanied by noodles and chilled chardonnay. They relished the spiciness of the dishes. Dining was a desirable entree to the evening's entertainment. She offered to pay but Tony laughed it off saying, “It’s a thank you present for you being you.”

She was never quite sure how to interpret what he said. Just as well he refused her attempt to pay, as her financial situation didn’t match up to her expensive tastes.

She wasn’t familiar with Southbank where the Festival Hall and many other iconic cultural centres were situated. Tony squeezed the car into the most unlikely of parking spaces and they completed the journey on foot along the bank of the Thames. The tickets Tony had been given were on the ground floor of the spacious, modern venue. She hadn’t expected his enthusiasm for a classical concert; well, so much the better for her.

People-watching was a satisfying experience after her quiet, sometimes secluded, country life. Moira watched the public file into their seats, noting contrasts in skin colour, body shape and size. Office workers still wore their business suits, others opted for casual slacks, a motley of T-shirts and rain jackets;

a mixture of individuals from all walks of life. Their energy would fuse together in their common love of the music, once the concert started.

Chatting filled the hall with a persistent murmur, then the members of the London Symphony Orchestra began to saunter in, occupying their designated seats on the stage, making themselves comfortable and testing their instruments, with the resulting cacophony of sound that obliterated human voices. The first violinist played an *A,* the standard for all instrument tuning, and the background noise of the hall began to decrease. The audience warmed up to the conductor and soloist, welcoming them with applause.

The lighting created an ambience suited to the lyrical qualities of the concerto. Once the pianist launched into playing, Moira abandoned her observing and analysing, to allow the music to embrace her and uplift her spirit. Despite feeling penniless, or maybe *because* she was pressed for money, she found herself appreciating this musical experience as never before.

At the end of the concert, Tony and she joined the crowd flocking out of the Festival Hall in contented mode. It had been a joyful interlude in her country life so punctuated by recent dramas, like ghosts. She felt refreshed.

On Sunday, Moira felt inspired to go back to the church to continue her exploratory sketches, taking a sketch book and charcoal this time. She returned to the vertical view she had enjoyed so much on the previous occasion. At this time of day, the trees and the church cast long shadows over the churchyard. All colour fused into dark and light, and Moira saw only form and structure. During the next couple of hours, she explored various approaches to shading. Immersed in her drawing, she lost all sense of time. There was only the now and the process of observing though sketching all of which renewed her energies.

After her drawing session, she appreciated her walk back to the cottage. It was as if the drawing process had improved her ability to see. The trees were a bright vibrant green that would appear unnatural in paintings. It was not just the result of a lot of rain; the chrome green of fresh buds heralded spring in England in a way that was never seen in the eucalyptus trees so common in New South Wales. There, the heat of the sun would rush this step of luscious new growth. In fact, the seasons were restricted to hot or cold, summer or winter. Here people had the time to embrace the change in the seasons, to enjoy spring and autumn. Perhaps this was a healthier option.

Mike continued to date Moira regularly. Then one day he suggested they go on holiday to Greece together. She had a sense that this holiday might catapult the relationship into a sexual one. Did she want that? So far she had managed to keep him at arm's length despite the magnetic attraction. Of course there had been holding hands and stolen kisses, but she had resisted anything more adventurous.

She didn't want infidelity to interrupt her current divorce process, which was so seamless at present. She wouldn't put it past Guido to hire a detective. The developing relationship with Mike needed some brakes. She remembered his arrival with a blonde woman at the English School barbecue. Of course that could have been a casual date, but who knows whether he was dating both of them simultaneously.

Where was she going to find the money to finance this trip? Was she going to use the capital she had squirrelled away in the bank? It was there for future emergencies. It might be weeks before the superannuation cheque arrived, and she had to be careful not to miss too much casual work, so the holiday would have to be one week rather than two.

"Mike, I would love to go, but with three conditions," she told him. "I pay for myself, no sex and only a week."

Insisting she pay for herself would be one way of keeping her independence. She would also be free to go off on her own if things got too steamy. This is when they had their first argument: Mike wanted her to go for two weeks. She found his sulking quite cute, and inwardly believed it might have to do with her rejection of sex. She had been right to insist on that. Separate bedrooms it would be.

The summer had been unpleasant because of frequent showers, creating humidity. She yearned for the warmth of the sun and the sea. She knew something about Greek culture. Melbourne in Australia was the third biggest Greek city in the world, and she had taught second generation Greek girls. But most of all she longed for the companionship Mike gave her.

They spent their time ferreting through brochures, deciding to take a package deal to the quiet island of Leros.

After a short flight, they arrived in Kos, where they were scheduled to take two ferries to Leros. At the second terminal, a large woman returning from her stay on Leros disembarked from the small boat they were waiting for. Mike and she exchanged bland greetings and *How are you*'s. Then Mike introduced Cindy to Moira, who was intrigued by the palpable embarrassment between the two of them, and later couldn't resist asking, "Who was that?"

Mike took his time before he finally said, "An old friend."

Moira turned her head away. There had to be more to that story; just as well she had decided on no sex. They clambered on to the boat. The sun penetrated the clouds and cast its rays over the churning sea. The islands were brown in colour; dry and without vegetation. The boat ripped through the choppy waves. The trip took her mind off Mike and – was it his girlfriend? Not a great beginning to a holiday. Too late to return now. Finally he asked, "Are you alright?"

She flicked her hair out of her eyes, adjusted her skirt, and glared at him, saying, "Perfectly alright."

"I suppose you're wondering about the woman we ran into. She means nothing to me."

"Mike, we are free agents happening to go on a holiday together. I'm fine with that."

"I came with her to this island last year."

"That's nice. I don't want to know about it."

"We didn't hit it off."

“Just let it go.”

They were like two individuals who hadn’t gelled with one another, each protecting personal boundaries. It was early days and Moira had made her position very clear. They would have an opportunity to get to know one another without sex complicating matters. She hoped he would allow her the space to swim and explore on her own if she so desired. Discovering the island by local bus might be fun. So what was the point of sharing a holiday with Mike? She wasn’t sure. Maybe it was more about togetherness.

Chapter 15

They arrived at their small hotel overlooking the bay and checked in. Moira could hear the waves breaking along the shore like soft breaths. She changed into her bikini, ran to the seashore and flung herself into the water, giving up all thoughts and embracing its silkiness. The blue water of the Aegean Sea sparkled like diamonds beneath the relentless sun. She felt the tightness of her muscles respond to the healing of the water. Her body released itself to the pleasure of swimming as she sought to soothe her inner aches. Some moments later Mike joined her.

They were still awkward with one another and they both held back from touching, probably the result of her *no sex* demand. Their snack consisted of *spanakorizo*, bought from a stall on the beach. She chewed the spinach and rice, which had been stewed slowly in lemon juice and oil. The spices were laced through the mixture, and local retsina was the perfect accompaniment to such home cooking. They both fell asleep on the beach. When they strolled along the beach later, she saw a fisherman slapping calamari on to the rocks, reminding her of Maroubra, a Sydney suburb, inhabited by second and third generation Greeks who did the same to tenderise the flesh.

White was an appropriate colour for the village buildings; easy to touch up and it reflected the sun's rays. The blue used for painting doors and window frames reinforced the colour of the ever-present sea, though the paint didn't wear as well. She imagined that by the end of the summer, the paint would be peeling off in layers, as if it had been bleached. And beside these man-made forms, the faded green olive trees writhed, struggling for survival in the sun-baked soil, now turned to dust. The cicadas in the heat of the late afternoon were conspicuous with the sound they made: a cross between crackling and humming.

In the evening, Moira and Mike were drawn to the music in the tavernas along the promenade. Coloured lights in each eating venue twinkled to the sound of the last of the straggling fishing boats returning to land. Waiters were touting for business along the pavements outside, and blackboard menus boasted a multitude of seafood dishes. As they strolled hand in hand along the promenade, she noticed a small taverna where there was a buffet counter with many cooked dishes, tempting with their smell, colour and texture. She recognised *moussaka*, a traditional casserole with eggplants, potatoes and minced meat topped with béchamel sauce. There were also *dolmades*, cooked minced meat mixed with rice, fresh herbs and seasonings, wrapped in vine leaves and served with egg lemon sauce, and of course the traditional salad with feta cheese. Images of eating at sophisticated Greek restaurants in Sydney came rushing back. This village however offered home cooking in all its simplicity, with fresh local produce. Moira craved calamari and salad, which she had frequently eaten in Sydney. Mike chose fish and salad. While waiting for their food they enjoyed fresh bread and *tzatziki*, a dip made of yoghurt, cucumber and garlic, accompanied by more retsina. It was as if they merged with the local culture by accepting food, the gifts of nature.

Eating the food was a sensory experience. The

tomatoes grown and ripened locally had the distinctive smell that supermarket tomatoes lacked. The Greeks upgraded simple fresh green beans to heights of gourmet sensory experience, creating *fasolakia*, when they slowly cooked them in a sauce. The fullest enjoyment of flavours was on the menu tonight.

Between forkfuls, Mike's thumb gently caressed the back of Moira's hands. His gaze rested on her breasts. The sensuality of the man sitting in front of her, fused with the seductiveness of the island, left her with emotions swirling. They were both visibly relinquishing the trappings of civilisation.

"The wind has a chill to it now. Shall we go?" said Mike.

"No," she cried. "We must try the baklava."

"What's that?"

"A rich, sweet pastry made up of paper-thin layers of filo pastry, interspersed with chopped nuts and honey. A dessert known for its richness and calories – food of the Gods – we must have it at least once."

Mike was willing to be enticed. However they both refused the traditional Metaxa brandy to go with it.

As they drew close to their apartment door, Mike turned her round to face him, brushed her lips softly with his lips, and ran his hands down the curves of her body. He traced a path of kisses from forehead to nose, lips and neck. He nibbled her ear. Finally she pulled away. Accepting her wishes, he unlocked the door.

Both of them had agreed to unwind by lazing for the first few days. Flaking out on sunbeds on the patio, they slept during the first day, then Mike rented a motorbike and bought a map from one of the shops. Packing their towels, hats and swimming gear in a backpack, they bought freshly baked bread, sweet-tasting tomatoes and feta cheese for lunch, and set off.

At first Moira felt nervous on the motorbike. It chugged along as if it might fall apart any moment, so she clung to Mike's back, wrapping her hands around his waist. As they climbed the hilly terrain, the road curved and the harbour came into view, with little white and blue houses overlooking it, sandy beaches beyond. She breathed in deeply when faced with the beauty of the local scene. They came across a Greek Orthodox church, and Mike pulled up nearby. The doors were unlocked, so, holding hands, they entered into the building. They admired the interior, which was decorated with Byzantine paintings, icons, marble and vitro windows, breaking the silence from time to time with their comments. Mike photographed details of the architecture, then they both sat down to sketch until it became sweltering hot, mid-afternoon.

They took off again, stopping at a deserted beach to have their belated lunch. Finding a sheltered spot under the pines, they spread their towels. Later, they splashed their way into the sea, alternatively swimming and cupping their hands to throw water at each other. Their laughter echoed around the silent cove. They jumped on to a wooden, deserted jetty, testing its strength.

The days bled into one another. Moira was acquiring a taste for the varied Greek ways of preparing food, for example, *yemista*, baked stuffed vegetables, as well as the charcoal-grilled and spit-roasted meats. They experimented with eating *tiropita*, cheese pie, for breakfast. It was freshly made every morning by the home bakery nearby, the smell wafting over in the freshness of the morning. Their days followed a relaxed routine that neither chafed nor pressured them. Leros was an unspoilt island; nature at its best. But at night Moira found herself tossing around restlessly on her bed.

The local Greeks told Mike and Moira about the disco on the other side of the island. Unsurprisingly it was called the *Hellenic*. Very Greek. Dancing started at 11:30 pm but they were advised to arrive after midnight. Once again, Mike hired a motorbike. This time they dressed in their glad rags. By now Moira had managed to buy some new clothes that were not traditionally embroidered, and both had acquired the bronzed look of the Greeks.

Mike found the way to the isolated building they had been told about. The pulsating rhythms were audible even before they reached the concrete building, which was surrounded by cars and motorbikes, parked in a haphazard, careless manner. The building was modern and fitted out with sophisticated audio equipment, which pounded away at high volume. A businessman had tapped into a need in Leros. They paid an entry fee, which included a cocktail. Moira was happy to test out the simple Greek phrases she had learnt: *kalispera*, meaning good evening and *efharisto,* meaning thank you. She recalled the disco she had been to in West Gidding, quite provincial when compared to this disco. There was nothing resembling village life about this set up; it was on a par with the best discos in Athens. Most of the dancers wore sophisticated outfits, usually leather, all young Greeks probably on holiday from the capital. Settled at their table with a drink in hand, they both watched the dancing.

Then Mike rose and picked up her hand and pulled her to the dance floor. They swung their way into vibrating to the music. While their passion for art had drawn them together, this holiday allowed them to share motorbikes, different music and food, and to create bonding.

Both of them enjoyed walking, and would frequently leave their hotel rooms for the day with a backpack. One day they had wandered up a steep, desolate hill, following an escarpment for several miles. To their surprise they arrived at a little valley with a single wooden house. They had to cross this valley to continue on their path so they descended to pass the building when a male voice hailed them with *kalimera.* They responded in kind, then their language skills dried up. Nonetheless, the elderly Greek motioned with his hand for them to sit down at the bench outside his house and went inside. Moments later, he emerged with a platter of washed grapes and offered them. They all nodded at each other while repeating *efharisto.* Moira was reminded of the generosity and warm-heartedness of the Greeks she had known in Sydney.

As Moira began to relax more, she slept better, enjoyed the open air life and laughed more openly. All the uptight tension of the arrival had dispersed, but it also brought the return journey closer.

On the second last evening, they were both sitting in the lounge chatting about their day when a loud noise from the upstairs apartment jolted them.

"What's going on?" began Moira.

They listened. The sound became repetitive. It sounded as if the bed upstairs was hitting the wall, in a rhythm that was speeding up. She and Mike locked eyes and they both burst out laughing.

"Do you want to join in?" Mike finally ventured with a seductive smile.

Moira ambled out on to the balcony, watching the sparkling sea, still laughing. Mike nuzzled his face into her shoulder. "Did you hear me?"

To his surprise, she said, "Oh, why not. I think it's a sign to enjoy ourselves."

She had longed to feel Mike's arms around her, to feel hugged. Mike stood behind her massaging her shoulders. "Are you sure?"

Then one hand moved round to the curve of her breast which he fondled, gently. She shivered with excitement. He moved round to face her, and held her chin so she had to gaze into his eyes. They contemplated each other, hearts beating in unison as the charcoal of evening deepened, while gathering white breakers boomed in the distance. She was like a moth attracted to light.

He then covered her mouth with his own, his tongue invading. His lips and hands explored her curves. He kissed her eyelids and behind her ears. His hands worked at the buttons of her blouse, loosening them, and fastened his mouth on her breast, sucking gently. The sensation left her moaning softly. She ruffled her fingers through his hair. Her skin tingled. They undressed each other tenderly. Clothes were peeled away and cast on the floor. The musky smell of his male body hovering over her overpowered her.

He lifted her and placed her on the bed. Her heart thudded.

"Do you like it this way?"

He traced his fingers along her inner thighs, slowly reaching the centre of her womanhood. Moira felt pulsating, warm sensations burst through her veins, with flickering bursts of pleasure. Then came his thrust, and he set off the rocking motion. They were both carried by the powerful tide of mounting passion, culminating in the explosion when body and soul became as one. They lay entwined but spent. It was a long time since she had been cherished in this way. Eventually sleep encompassed them both.

Next morning they woke up refreshed, swam in the sea and sat on the balcony enjoying their orange juice and Greek yoghurt. The thick local coffee was best in a taverna, so they ambled down to the promenade in search of one, holding hands.

"What about getting a motorbike again? We can visit another deserted beach," said Moira.

Returning to the sheltered coastline they had discovered previously, they fell into each other's arms and merged with a timeless kiss. He claimed her lips, discarded her bikini, and kissed her now-familiar body with greater urgency. Their lovemaking took on greater passion as they fused into oneness. Then they cooled off in the sea water before setting off on their return journey.

The rest of the short time left was spent lazing,

a shorthand for enjoying each other in newly-found physical ways, seeking bodily pleasures. They interspersed their sun-bathing, swimming and making love on this romantic island with forays to the tavernas to build up their energies.

While returning to the UK the way they came, by ferry and plane, Mike read his book while Moira pondered. She was uncertain about the wisdom of her recent actions. She was aware she was a married woman, even though she had initiated her divorce. She saw Mike put his book down and pick up her hand, pressing his lips to her palm.

"I have a proposition for you," he said.

"Yes?'

"I think you should move in with me." He kissed her hand again, "No pressure. Just think about my suggestion."

Back at the cottage in West Gidding, an airmail envelope lay on the dresser at the entrance hall to Moira's room. She recognised her lawyer's address on the back. Liz must have updated him with her latest address. She hoped it was good news. On opening it, a plain, sealed envelope fell out. The accompanying note from her lawyer explained that the letter from Guido was being forwarded to her. Her stomach muscles clenched. Sometimes she felt she was leading two parallel lives: the new in its embryonic form, and the old, which interrupted, and sometimes threatened, the new order. She began reading the letter.

My Darling Moira

I was utterly devastated to return home from my business trip to find you gone. You were blunt in the note you left for me. Nonetheless we are still married and you are still very much my wife.

I would like to know why you found our marriage so unhappy. We have been together for ten years. You've been free to work, paint, travel, meet up with your friends.

OK, I understand you may have been upset by my affair but I'm not the first husband to have one, and does one mistake end the marriage that has worked for us all this time?

It's not too late to change your mind. I would welcome you back to Sydney with open arms. I've even reserved a table at our favourite restaurant for a wedding anniversary celebration on your return.

Hoping to hear from you,

With all my love,

Guido

Moira wasn't interested in his logical, conciliatory, supercilious tone, or elastic truth. Of course he only saw the situation from his point of view. Moira didn't like his allusion to still being *his wife* as if he owned her with a marriage certificate. The marriage was over. That's why she had been brief in her note.

Anyone reading his letter would describe it as rational, logical, and psychologically clever. Living with him, she had experienced him as volatile, unpredictable, and unreliable. From the perspective of distance, she saw that in some way she had been reliving her mother's life, with the view that marriage was for life, no matter how difficult the path. She now understood that one of the reasons which had blocked her from making a break earlier was lack of confidence in her worth. This had always made it easier for Guido to play with her emotions.

His blatant infidelity gave her the excuse for leaving him. He didn't seem to realise she had a choice, and she'd made it. Of course she was a coward for choosing writing rather than a face-to-face meeting, but even her parents saw that as being wise. She would embrace her freedom. It had taken long enough to reach that point of no return; no more procrastination.

She changed into her clothes to go walking. Pounding her feet on the pavement helped to remove the built up tension, the impatience with Guido, the anger at his ignoring her wishes. She had always known he would try to bind her to him, and in many ways she had allowed this to happen. No one was going to make her go back now. He hadn't mentioned contacting her friends, and she hoped he would leave her parents alone. As she continued pacing out the miles, the tight seals on the past were straining. Images filtered from the past. She needed to talk to someone.

On returning to number 36, she rang Scarlett to set up a coffee meeting at *The George*. As soon as Scarlett arrived, she announced, “I’ve received a letter from Guido via my lawyer.”

“Tell me what’s it all about?”

“It’s the churning emotions it brought up for me…”

“Go on. Out with it.”

“In the second year of their marriage, we were having a heated argument about Guido’s flirting. He felt I had accused him unfairly, and bristled with anger. The angry tones grew louder. Then out of the blue, he slapped my face. I was in shock. It was so unexpected.” Moira found herself reliving the scene, her heart-rate rising. She shuddered as she remembered the shock of his hand crashing into her cheek. He had forced her head back against the wall, and his breath had smelled of alcohol.

"Then as quickly as he had struck me, he released his hold on me and left the apartment." She remembered how she lay on the sofa, inert and humiliated, putting her fingers to her fast-swelling cheek. "Next day, a friend of mine advised me to report to my local doctor, and ask to be examined, so the abuse could be recorded in my medical records."

"A good idea," Scarlett interjected.

"The doctor checked my bruising and acknowledged I was still in shock. What perplexed me was that he said to think very carefully before leaving Guido."

"So what did you do?"

"I rented a room from a friend for a couple of months. Guido persisted in trying to contact me. He said he was horrified at his own behaviour."

"I should think so."

"He promised it would never happen again. What really bothered me was that he would turn up at my school wanting to see me. It was embarrassing. "

"So did you see him?"

"I spoke to older women whom I trusted, and

they too, advised me not to rush with decisions. Eventually Guido wore me down with persuasive promises and I agreed to give the relationship a second chance."

Moira stopped and took a couple of sips of her coffee, calming herself down from her physical response to the recollections.

"When we started living under the same roof again, we took out a mortgage to buy an apartment, acting as if everything had returned to normal. But I was careful to avoid confrontation, especially when Guido had been drinking. More importantly, the shame of being hit overshadowed the relationship for me."

"So how do you feel now?"

"Guido's letter has reminded me of this incident, and upset me."

"Moira, go for a walk, or go home and pamper yourself with a good book and a bubble bath. You've got it off your chest. That's important." Scarlett felt like adding that she should see a therapist but that could wait to a more appropriate time. "Come on, I'll drive you home."

"I'm OK. Acknowledging this past experience, and sharing it, has helped. I'll walk home. It will help me sleep."

They said goodbye, Scarlett hugging Moira and patting her back.

As she strode down the road, Moira realised she had kept her secret so well that she had erased it from her mind as if it had never taken place. The reality was that she had been in denial. Her sense of worth had been diminished by the experience

She stopped outside West Gidding, sat on a wall under some beeches, and wept for the lost years. What choked her up was that she couldn't forgive herself for continuing her life with Guido. She needed to follow in Scarlett's footsteps and go into therapy, but for that, she needed money.

On Monday, Moira's day was shattered by the arrival of a telegram:

MA IN INTENSIVE CARE STOP MASSIVE HEART ATTACK STOP LOVE PA

Chapter 16

Shock numbed Moira. More than that, she wanted to be by her mother's side. Ma would have been disappointed she had not visited them before leaving Australia, and now was the time to redress the situation, to act quickly. She rang Tony and Zara, giving both the same information: "Just received a telegram. My mother had a heart attack and is in intensive care in hospital. Am going over to Australia as soon as I can get a seat on the plane."

Mike's phone remained silent and the answering service took no messages. The news had churned her up; her panic went into overdrive, and her heart thumped wildly. She would need to get a seat on the first available flight to Australia. It would have to be an international flight to Sydney followed by a domestic flight to Adelaide. She could leave the decision of whether to stay in Sydney to the return journey, and opted for a two week stay in Australia.

When she phoned TRAILFINDERS they offered her a seat on the Tuesday evening flight.

Luckily, her credit card had arrived from the bank a few days earlier, so she paid for the ticket over the phone. Her concern about how the credit would be paid off would have to wait for another day. Once the flight was booked, she rang her father to pass on her arrival details for Adelaide. She discerned a relief in the tone of his voice. The latest news was that her mother was still in intensive care, but in a stable condition.

She threw some essentials into a carry-all that Scarlett had loaned her, and forced herself to read the books Scarlett had brought. Still no response from Mike. Tony didn't have the time to drop her off at the airport but offered to book her one of the vehicles he used for airport pick- ups, for which she was grateful.

On the plane, sleep eluded Moira. So here she was on an intercontinental flight again, in the opposite direction to the one she had taken almost two months ago. She had a niggling feeling that returning to Australia was in some way taking a step backwards. It was breaking her positive momentum of settling into West Gidding, yet she knew she had to see both her parents – and now.

Too nervous to drive, her father said he would take a taxi to meet her at the airport, and they would go straight to the hospital. Moira wondered if worry was depriving him of sleep.

Her mother had experienced high blood pressure from her pregnancy days and lived with angina since the age of thirty-six. Her personality was to push herself to the limit, with regular two-day migraines to attest to that. She had an indefatigable will; surely she would survive. For Moira, not knowing the outcome was the worst part.

Because of the demands of her career and living in Sydney, Moira had been conspicuous by her absence at many family events that her mother had initiated. At recent reunions with her parents, she had been aware of how they had bonded together in their frailty. They were fiercely independent, and fought hard to keep their home and lifestyle, though age had slowed them down. After the years of crises and dramas, they now supported each other; their dependence on each other mellowed the once-dynamic conflicts. Finally Moira took the sleeping tablets she had brought with her.

She was groggy when she arrived at Kingsford Smith International Airport in Sydney and transferred to the domestic terminal to catch the plane for Adelaide. She felt impatient to be at her journey's end.

At the airport in Adelaide, her eyes scanned the small crowd waiting for the arrivals. Moira couldn't see her father at first, then realised he was the small shrunken figure at the side. He hugged her, gripping her tightly, then started to gabble. "Ma crumpled on to the floor clutching her chest. I was in shock but knew I had to act. My hands were shaking, but I managed to call the ambulance. They took her away for evaluation and treatment. I wanted to go with Ma in the ambulance but the medics asked me to go to bed and gave me a tranquiliser."

For a quiet man, he had developed a need to talk, a sure sign he was anxious about her mother's condition.

When Moira arrived at the hospital she was

aware of the strong antiseptic smell and the nurses scurrying along the corridors attending to patients in different wards. She was taken to her mother's room by her father. Moira's rubber-soled shoes squeaked on the polished linoleum floor. When they entered Ma's room, the nurse discreetly tiptoed out. Moira crept in and surveyed the scene. Digital monitors blinked at her. In their midst, her once vibrant and energetic mother lay listlessly, as white as the walls around her. She had difficulty in breathing.

Moira's stomach was churning over as she stepped towards her mother's still form. She pulled up a chair on one side and took her mother's hand. A monitoring device was secured to her other hand, and both were thin, veined, and peppered with brown age spots, which the sun had brought out, when she had worked many hours at establishing her beloved garden. Moira noted the sagging posture her father had assumed on the other side of the bed. The fear of loss was palpable.

Memories embraced Moira. She visualised her mother helping her with oral French homework.

School holidays spent by the beach. If Moira returned home from school in tears for any reason, Ma had always been a source of comfort. Ma sewing her first party dress, all floating gauze and frills. The excitement of dressing up to go to see *Holiday on Ice* with her before Christmas one year. Following Ma's instructions for preparing festive dishes at Christmas and licking out the cake mixture bowls. That, best of all. Moira was unaware of time passing.

"Ma you are strong. You are a survivor. I love you," she whispered.

The silence in the room was broken when the cardiac specialist arrived, his face grave as he checked the records at the end of the bed. "She's weak but her condition is stable. She's been sedated and will sleep comfortably through till the morning."

Moira mentally debated whether to stay by her mother's side overnight. She observed her father. Never an active person, he seemed to be dwarfed by her mother's illness, lost without the presence of her enormous energy. Moira decided to go home with her father. They both needed a decent meal – hospital snacks were no substitute and the week would be a long one.

On the way home to Westbourne Park, a suburb of middle class sprawling bungalows, they stopped at a supermarket, where Moira bought juices, vegetables and fish. She bought wine for herself. It was a long time since she had drunk the Barossa Valley brands from local vineyards, and she wondered whether the Barossa Valley had changed much since the days of her youth. The German shops and Lutheran churches from the turn of the twentieth century must still be operating in the small towns. Her father preferred beer so she placed some small bottles into her wheelie.

When they reached home, Moira asked her father to put some classical music on. Many years before, he had played the violin, but was forced to give it up because of a tumour in his neck. She set about preparing the meal, while her father started up a fire in the lounge, as the winter evenings were nippy. Sitting down in the kitchen with her, he started talking about how he and Ma had met, as if memories would give him the strength to tide him over the period of Ma's debilitated state of health.

Moira didn't dare have him peeling anything. Cut fingers would involve more visits to the hospital, which she wasn't ready to face. He watched her cook the fish in white wine, and steam the vegetables, a complete contrast to his style of frying food. At least it was a healthy option and gave them a chance to converse.

They dined, and Pa continued to talk about his life with Ma. The fish was tender and fragrant, mixed with the sweetness of garlic. Each forkful satisfied their taste buds, however the combination of wine, warmth and jet-lag made her sleepy. She would deal with the washing up in the morning, she decided, opting to retire early.

Waking up after a satisfying sleep, Moira allowed herself some time to ponder. It was strange returning to Australia. Adelaide was the most English of all the Australian cities, more akin to West Gidding. The city had been planned, and never played host to a convict settlement. It seemed quieter than Sydney or

Melbourne, which were more noisy, more cosmopolitan and somehow the pace was faster.

Her tough measures to cut Guido out of her life had been shattered with having to return to Australia prematurely, and she wondered whether she should spend time in Sydney on the way back. Shuddering, she wiped the thought from her mind. It was time to breakfast and make her way to the hospital with her father.

When Mike returned home from Leros, he had been ecstatic. It had been an idyllic holiday. Checking his landline messages, he picked up several hysterical messages from Margaret, then nothing for two days. Next, Margaret's doctor left a message, asking Mike to contact him urgently. Mike craved Moira's presence to calm him down. When he called her, Pat Myles had answered the phone with the news that Moira had just left for Heathrow to fly out to Australia. Apparently Moira's mother was in intensive care in Adelaide after a massive heart attack. What a blow. The pain of missing Moira before her departure was like a sudden bolt.

Ma had slept through the night and, though weak, was able to ask a few questions about Moira's arrival back in Adelaide. Moira hoped her mother would listen the doctor's advice to rest and slow her life down. Ma asked her about the UK, then she rested her head on the pillow, her body slack and limp, such a contrast to her usual energetic self. Moira and her father dragged themselves to their feet and Moira took his elbow guiding him to the hospital café for a coffee. They spent the first week following the same pattern every day: Moira drove her father to the hospital and stayed with both of them until late afternoon when she and her father returned home to eat.

Pa kept repeating how grateful he was for her visit and her help. Moira felt that the evening talks were allowing him to relax. He began to sleep better and on the way to the hospital, he started asking about her art. Moira accepted it was his way of reconnecting with her after so many years of her living in Sydney.

His drawing skills were outstanding and it was he who had encouraged her to follow her passion for it later in life. It seemed important for her to accept his comments, if not accolades, for the art work she did. Enrolled at the East Sydney Tech, and the Julian Ashton School of painting in Sydney in recent years, she had revitalised her drawing and painting skills, and knew her worth.

Moira had returned to be by her mother's side, but her mother's illness had brought her closer to her father. When was the last time she had spent meaningful time with her father? The bonds of love were reconnecting her with Pa as never before.

Another evening, Moira's father talked about the history of his family, revealing that his grandparents had lived near Horsham in West Sussex.

"Why have you never told me that before?" Moira said. Perhaps her attraction to England came from her genes.

"Well, Miss Independence you were not around much after your University days. Would you have even been interested?"

Moira recalled how secretive she had been about her departure from Sydney. She hadn't wanted to speak to her parents. Shame and guilt clouded her memories.

"I see what you mean. The marriage to Guido was not without its problems," she ventured.

"Before you say anything more, your mother and I thought it was not the most ideal of unions. However, we accepted your choice of partner."

Moira wondered how much they knew. She didn't know whether she was ready to talk about her marriage.

"You know, you remind me of my mother," her father said. "She went back to England, but lived in London." No wonder Moira was taken with this city. It was in her blood. "That's where she met your grandfather. Once children came along she thought they would have a better life in Australia, and so they gathered their financial resources and settled here. Of course I, too, returned to England, only to bring you all back here again."

Moira considered her liking for West Sussex in

the light of all this new information.

“Are you aware of any remaining family in West Sussex?” Perhaps she would be able to visit them. Also tracing records was growing in popularity in the UK.

“You know me. I’m not so good at writing letters. Your mother enjoys that. As you know yourself, much of our family life was intertwined with building up our business – a never ending scenario.”

Before he retired, her father had been a consulting engineer, and his small business had made inroads to their family life on many an occasion during her adolescence. At that moment the phone rang. It sounded harsh breaking into the intimacy of their conversation. Concerned about the possibility of bad news from the hospital, she jumped up in a hurry and stumbled. Assuming that something was wrong showed Moira how stressed she was. A few rings later, she grabbed the receiver.

“Hello.”

The line was crackling. It wasn’t a local call.

Moira was relieved.

"Hello," she said again.

"It's me, Tony. Is everything alright?" he said.

"As well as could be expected under the circumstances."

Moira fell into the rhythm of chatting to Tony. She welcomed his interest and caring. His school was still attracting large numbers of students. Zara was preoccupied with insurance claims, Felicity wanted a divorce and Scarlett was going out with Charles. He didn't mention Mike.

"I'm really grateful for your call and all the news," she said.

Listening to Tony reminded her of her other life that was still in embryonic form, but nonetheless real. It was news that also served as light relief to all the anxiety around her mother's illness. Tony ended the call by saying he would ring again.

Moira had always sensed her parents didn't think Guido was good enough for her but had accepted her choice. She put the kettle on, prepared the tea cups and made the tea. They sat at the same kitchen table that must have presided over many shared confidences. Taking a deep breath, she took the plunge, “What did you and Ma really think about my marriage?”

Her father sipped his tea, put the cup down and said, “Your mother and I agreed that Guido had a very pleasant social veneer, but feared his underlying aggressiveness might harm you.”

A little nerve trembled at Moira’s temple.

“What concerned me was he might be controlling you with his anger.”

Moira remained silent.

“We couldn’t say anything when you made your choice to marry Guido. He would have resented interference, and there was a chance he might vent his anger on you because of our involvement.”

Moira had to admit she had kept her distance from her parents deliberately to hide from the shame she felt when he assaulted her.

“Good for you to take the decision to leave him. The UK trip happened at the right time.”

She smoothed out her skirt. Memories forget

details such as names, but the emotions associated with the past are never forgotten. Her feelings tumbled over one another. She might as well continue.

"When Guido cooked me his weekend breakfasts and brought flowers for no special reason in the early years, I was more patient with him. Then came his lack of success with business. As I saw it, he had innovative ideas but lacked the perseverance to finish off details."

"Yes, I would guess that Guido was more interested in social connections, working in sales, rather than focussing on the self-discipline required for goal setting and planning a business. If you managed to live with all that, what led you to leaving him recently?"

Chapter 17

She covered her face with her hands and finally croaked, "I caught him with another woman in our bed."

She had spat it out. It was a relief for her to talk about it. Her father, never one for showing his emotions, put his arms around her and hugged her, which triggered the pent-up tears. He allowed her to sob out the past. When the weeping ceased, he said, "We only learn through our mistakes. Now I understand why leaving Australia improved your chances of cutting off from Guido."

She, in turn, was relieved to have his support.

"Just a moment," he said and went out of the kitchen. He returned, holding two cut glasses with a large amount of brandy in each.

"Have one of these. It will do you good." Moira took a sip and coughed, choking over the burning at the back of her throat.

"You know, the right partner makes you feel that you could be a better person than you ever imagined."

Moira gaped at her father, open-mouthed, her thoughts recalling the numerous occasions her parents had argued vociferously. Had those disagreements faded into the distant mists of the past?

"Loving someone does not mean you agree with them all the time or let them organise your life for you," he continued. "Your mother is a very strong woman, a survivor. She had a difficult life, and always reacted to situations by fighting for her rights as she saw them."

Moira stared at her father. He had never opened up so much with her before, but she could now understand her mother better. Ma had a very strong personality, a real whirlwind, surpassing Zara in colour and drive; she had always been the driving force behind her family.

"Don't you remember when you came with a broken nose from school because some boy had dashed into you? Well, if the surgeon had had his way, your twisted nose would have stayed with you until your body had stopped growing; another five years. It was your mother who fought for your immediate operation."

"I don't remember her standing up for me."

"You were probably unaware of it, on that occasion – you were only ten. You remind me of her, with your inner strength."

"All I remember is we didn't really groove together very well."

"Aha…proof that you were too similar."

After a few more sips of brandy, Moira's head started swimming. "You know Pa, I know you are encouraging me to drink this stuff but I think I'm getting tipsy."

"You should sleep much better tonight. We can always talk some more tomorrow."

Pa insisted he reimburse Moira for her ticket to Australia. Pride would not stand in the way of her accepting his gesture. One day she would be able to pay back her debt, when the superannuation money arrived.

Tony continued to ring every few days. Not only did he fill in with the news but he gave Moira a sense of continuity with her life in England.

Her father was pleased to see Moira relaxing more. Once Moira's mother was out of intensive care, she steadily improved. Ma was a survivor. Moira was instrumental in setting up carers for her mother's future convalescence at home, and she also arranged for a person to come in and cook for her parents. When Moira shared her concerns about not being there for her mother when she came home, Pa was adamant she needed to return to her new life.

"We will manage with the extra help you have arranged."

"Are you going to stay in Sydney on the way back?" her father asked one day after they returned from the hospital.

"I just don't know whether I have the nerve."

"Maybe you should stay a couple of days, arrange a proper farewell with your friends. It would give you some closure." Closure. Since when had her father used psychological terms? She said she would think about it.

Later she mulled the idea over. Guido didn't know Liz. She had been successful before in keeping her plans secret so this time was no different. Her father was right. She would spend a couple of nights in Sydney. It would be fun.

Like most Australian men on a Friday evening, Guido closed the week by going to the local pub, a ritual for unwinding before the weekend. The steak and vegetables were worth eating there. He couldn't remember whether he had eaten breakfast, and lunch was a hamburger. He had missed Moira's cooking, which was healthier, but had to accept the reality of his situation. His relationship with Rebecca had ended, as he felt she was too needy. Being single gave him infinite freedom but little satisfaction, and he still felt the humiliation of Moira leaving him. As he headed for the toilets, he recognised a group of teachers from Moira's school. He doubted they would remember him, especially in the half-light of the lounge, but he didn't feel like talking to any of them anyway. As he passed the screen between the group and the toilets, he thought he heard the words, “Moira’s in Sydney.”

His brain exploded with the extra blood that had started pumping. He halted abruptly and bent down to tie a shoe lace.

“How come?”

“Her mother in Adelaide had a heart attack. She’s on her way back to the UK, stopping in Sydney for a couple of days.”

“How do you know?” someone called out.

“I heard Liz talking on the phone to someone.”

Inner pain clawed at Guido. His feelings spiralled out of control. His eyes now contained fury as sharp as razor blades. He couldn’t hear the chorus of reason.

When Liz met Moira at Kingsford-Smith International Airport, they were both speaking at the same time, breaking into each other’s conversation as if life was only to be enjoyed. Moira chided herself for her former hesitation. Life was on the crest of a wave again.

“No doubt I created enough sensation when I

resigned from my job," said Moira, hoping she had been forgiven by her colleagues for her departure, and the problems at school that she had inadvertently caused. Liz was driving back to the Eastern suburbs, where she had moved into some of the most expensive real estate in Sydney.

"Where would you like to go now?" said Liz. She had noticed Moira's softened features.

"Bondi Beach. Let's go to the bookshop, where we can buy a cappuccino."

She felt like a driver who needed to return to driving as soon as possible after an accident. It had to be back to the old haunts for her, though she refused to return to her home suburb. She didn't want to run into Guido. Liz found a parking place and they walked the rest of the distance. A pity about August being winter in Sydney. In Queensland she would have swum, though the locals would have considered her crazy; here the water was too cold. Nevertheless the views of the sea compensated for not swimming. She would celebrate her arrival by having chocolate torte with her coffee. This time she would say farewell with dignity.

Liz had phoned close friends and some teaching colleagues inviting them to dinner at a Greek restaurant. In the evening, when Liz and she arrived, friends were thronging, bouzouki music was competing with laughter and conversation, and greetings were filled with *ohs* and *ahhs*. The person she least expected to come was her former boss, the Principal of her school, Rod Brown. He greeted her warmly and said he would give a short speech after the entrée, then slip out quietly, as he had another engagement later on. When he stood up, he spoke glowingly of her achievements, but most of all, he praised her for following the path of her heart's desire. That brought tears to Moira's eyes and clapping from the attendees.

As the noise escalated, she recalled her most recent enjoyment of Greek culture with Mike in Leros. The food in the restaurant was as authentic as in Greece. The evening was livening up; line dancing was beginning. Her steps moved in the rhythms that had become familiar to her over the years.

It was a sunny morning. Liz had gone to the gym and Moira sat in the back garden and allowed the sun to penetrate her body with warmth. Both front and back doors were opened. She was lulled into a nostalgic frame of mind as she thought of the pleasant images from yesterday's event. Just aware of the soft radio music in the background, she fell into a semi doze on the wooden garden chair.

A prickling sensation climbed up her spine as if someone was watching her. She opened her eyes. There was Guido leaning against the wall. Cool and detached, measuring her with his intense gaze. His eyes were semi-closed, lizard-style. She froze.

"So how is my darling wife?"

The dulcet tones contrasted with the sarcastic enunciation. Moira was too nonplussed to reply; she felt suspended in time. There was tight knot in her chest, and when she opened her mouth to speak, no voice emerged. Her body felt paralysed with fear. She placed her hands on the arms of the chair in an effort to rise from it. The wooden back of the deckchair rattled against the stone wall, and Guido came over, pushing her back into it, then backed away again.

"No need to get up. So was I the cause of your unhappy marriage?" he said. "I would like to hear the answer from your own lips."

She felt threatened, but to buy time, kept talking to him.

"How did you know I was here?"

"You think your movements haven't been followed? It's no problem to hire a private detective."

"Have you been stalking me?"

"Don't be cute with me. Answer my first question."

"I am not going to be cross-examined by you or anybody else."

She got up quickly. He took three steps across the terrace, lurched towards Moira and whipped his hand across her face. The crack of the slap startled her as much as his action. It sounded like a whip. She could smell the stench of onions and garlic on his breath. He launched into a volley of words, "You thought you could just walk out on me when you felt like it?"

He yanked her hair sharply and slammed her head against the back wall of the building. A thin thread of spittle emerged from her lips. "You thought I would never find out about you sneaking off to Britain."

Moira failed to disengage herself from him; his grip was like a vice. She tried to bite Guido's hand but missed. He pulled back her head and thrust it against the wall again. She felt the metallic taste of blood running from her nose. She heard herself moaning like some animal. The blood was dripping down the back of her throat and she spluttered. She tried to get into a vertical position to avoid choking on the blood. Dizziness stopped her struggling. It was easier to give in. She slumped to the floor, her body sliding down the wall. Then oblivion took over...she sank into unconsciousness...

Chapter 18

Fluorescent lights. Sharp stabs of pain. Moira's throat felt swollen. Swallowing was difficult. Her skull felt shattered. Where was she? Something was wrong. Her eyes wouldn't budge beyond a slit. Someone gently touched her arm.

"You'll be fine," said a soft voice.

Moira tried to speak but only a rasping sound emerged.

"You're in Darlinghurst Hospital. Don't worry, your friends brought you here yesterday morning. You have to rest." She drifted off.

She woke up again later, unaware that tears were seeping out of her eyes. The nurse explained that a policeman wanted a statement from her. Moira panicked. She was supposed to be returning to the UK. What day was it? The nurse calmed her down and said she would be fine to go back to her friend's next morning. It was better for her to stay under medical supervision for the night. The police took a short statement regarding the identity of her assailant, and thanked her. Abject because she had lost her sense of dignity, Moira relied on her body cells to remember how to function, and was relieved to escape into the land of sleep again. When she woke up, the light had changed. The room was filled with the dusky pink of the setting sun, at odds with the mix of anger and shame that she felt.

Liz arrived in the evening

"What happened yesterday?" Moira asked.

"We found you collapsed in the courtyard. Rod Brown wanted to give you some flowers as an apology for leaving so early. I met him on the doorstep minutes after a man ran out of the house. We made our way to the courtyard at the back and saw the blood around you. Rod was on the ball, ringing for the ambulance within seconds, contacting the police and making a statement. A restraining order will be issued against Guido."

Moira was about to bombard her with questions, but Liz continued.

"We were lucky to have come upon you so

quickly. This was early yesterday morning. The hospital emergency staff checked you out when you got here, and treated you for shock, and bruises on your face and head. They were worried about you having concussion, but your head must be made of sterner stuff as you passed all the tests.

"Oh no," groaned Moira.

"I think you should listen to the doctor and stay here one more night. He says you will feel much better tomorrow and should be able to leave in the afternoon. I'll pick you up. If you like, I can pack your bag and we can go straight to the airport from the hospital."

"Let me think about it."

"In the meantime, make the most of your rest. Do you want me to ring your father?"

"Please don't worry him," she whispered.

Next morning, the nurse on duty lectured her: "A violent person always has good intentions to reform but those feelings are short-lived. Their past of being hurt, or badly done by, always catches up with them."

Moira just nodded, wincing as her head ached anew.

"And don't forget you're not responsible for your husband's actions."

Moira remembered reading in her psychology course that women who have a lot of responsibility in childhood attracted weaker men who were unable to give them love. Was that her problem? Maybe she had wanted to save him from himself. Or was it that her quieter nature appeared weak to him?

Moira tossed about in the night. Mistakes are the great turning points in our lives. They were like signposts if we paid attention to them. If we learned from them, we became stronger. Well, she'd become accustomed to his angry outbursts. She'd been in denial about his previous assault. So Guido must have been following her. Once a woman-basher, always a woman-basher. Guido couldn't just dominate her with the back of a hand.

Liz had brought Moira's make up kit to the hospital. Tablets had reduced the swelling on her face, and Liz applied the make up over the bruises before she checked out of the hospital. Sunglasses completed the disguise – she was anxious to protect herself from prying eyes. On the plane she wore her slumber shade. Moira was still struggling with the shock that she had been beaten up in revenge.

Moira was relieved she had achieved her closure in Australia this time, spent the couple of weeks with her parents and said goodbye to her friends who had been her support for all those years, but she returned to the UK nursing physical and emotional bruises. Her dark blue facial bruises could be covered with concealer; the inner bruises would take time to heal.

Arriving at Heathrow, Moira waited for the immigration officer's reaction to her Australian passport. She didn't have the appetite for confrontation so she kept silent. He gave her a visa for six months. How could she have panicked about a visa so much in May? What a waste of energy.

Although she had been desperate to leave Australia, she wasn't so sure of her motives for returning and staying in West Gidding now. Previously it had been a challenge, a promise of a new life. She had lost the feeling of optimistic expectation somewhere. She returned feeling restless, disoriented, and she dragged herself like an old woman struggling to keep her painful arthritic limbs on the move. She felt she had fallen victim to her body's bruises in more ways than one.

As Scarlett was working, Tony came to the airport to collect her. He refrained from asking too many questions. Wearing a cap with a sun visor that kept her face in shadow, she peered out of the car window listlessly. She could hardly believe that the fresh green fields of spring, which she had experienced on arrival in the UK, were now replaced with sandstone-beige, neatly ploughed, dried soil where the wheat had been cut. Large rolls of hay were grouped in different parts of the fields. The end of summer must have been dry to harvest so early.

When she arrived home, a letter in the official brown envelope was waiting for her. She expected it to contain news from the Home Office. Her concentration was poor, so she would leave opening the letter till she had rested. Then her memories flared up again, bringing a sudden reminder of the violence in Sydney. The images from the past punched her in the stomach. She couldn't forgive and forget. Luckily her teeth hadn't been knocked out.

Moira was still resolute in her desire to paint. In fact, it was the only occupation to take her thoughts away from the events of the recent past. She found that when she painted, her anxiety dissipated. Frequently she found herself stopping in the middle of a piece of work, then tearing it up.

Moira was longing for comforting hugs. Mike was silent. No contact. Was the Leros experience just a passing interlude for him? Eventually he made a brief call, but seemed distracted when he spoke, even distant. His behaviour was a disappointment, after the emotional intensity of the holiday.

Maybe the romantic holiday memories needed to be replaced by reality. She liked Mike's debonair, sophisticated exterior. They shared much in common but there was also a lick of uncertainty that left her feeling insecure. The chemistry between Mike and herself reminded her of the excitement with Guido in the first days, and where did that lead to? Maybe she was transferring the memories of the attack she had sustained in Sydney. She constantly compared Mike with Guido, her eyes opening up to the person Mike was. The intensity of their relationship created a tension not conducive to inner peace.

In contrast to Mike, Tony persisted in trying to cheer her up with his jokes. His mischievous comments still elicited a laugh from her. Sometimes they went to the pub. The companionable routine protected her from thinking too deeply.

She hadn't seen Scarlett in the weeks leading up to the Leros trip, so when Scarlett suggested meeting up for coffee, she agreed.

"I met Charles again at another art exhibition in Henley when you left for Australia. We clicked and have been going out and spending a lot of time together."

Moira listened. She was happy for Scarlett but didn't have the energy to be enthusiastic.

"The relationship feels just spot on," Scarlett said. "You were right. When Fate brings us events, decision making is easier."

Both Scarlett and Charles were undergoing divorce processes, getting closer to each other romantically, and planning a future together. How could a couple of weeks bring about such changes? Secretly Moira thought Scarlett was perhaps replacing one man with another, without the breathing space required to own herself as a woman on her own.

August in the eastern part of England brought some more dry, hot weather. Moira felt sticky and sweaty, that no amount of showering relieved. Tony continued to ask her to do some teaching sessions but her heart wasn't in it. Then one day she received a short letter from her father. She hurriedly opened it as if to stall any unpleasant news.

Hello Pet,

A surprise for you that I'm writing? Well, you know me. I'm going to keep this short. Ma is doing very well after her wake up call. Slowly but surely.

She's even trying to persuade me to go to England with her. Now that would be something! We've started talking about that possibility. It would be better to come before your winter to miss the cold. Alternatively we could come in late spring. Let me know what you think might work best for you.

I have enclosed a newspaper cutting that I came across unexpectedly. Thought you might be interested. It seems that your ex (not officially as your divorce has not come through) has got himself engaged.

Hope you are doing just fine. Keep up the painting.

Love

Pa

Well, well. Fancy Pa getting pen to paper. Moira was pleased to hear her mother was doing well, and a trip to look forward to? She unfolded the newspaper cutting. It was taken from a cycling news article. She scanned the newspaper fragment for Guido's name. There it was. He was engaged to Liz

Curtis, her former colleague and friend. Oh my…There was no accounting for people's tastes! Well Liz was welcome to him. She was young. Maybe they would be happy. Guido's life no longer touched her, his actions no longer upset her. She must be moving forward.

Chapter 19

A few weeks later, Moira's superannuation cheque arrived, instilling her life with a new energy. Her first impulse was to hijack some of the funds for regular counselling sessions with Scarlett's therapist.

The words spilt from her mouth like lava from a volcano. In examining the memories of her family life, she reclaimed lost pieces of herself. Moira learned about her fear of not succeeding enough. Much of her childhood had been spent pleasing her parents. Their approval had been equated with love, at least in her mind. Later, she followed her parents' choice of career instead of her own. There was also the ever-complex, ever-puzzling acceptance of Guido's abuse. She sometimes spent hours in her consciousness trying to decipher the reasons for her apathetic acceptance. Her therapist encouraged Moira to forgive herself and to consciously develop the habit of pleasing herself.

By coincidence, one evening brought her into contact with shopping, West Sussex style – an ideal opportunity to practice her new habit. It transpired that a little van arrived in West Gidding a few times a year, packed with exclusive brands of women's clothing from London, with discounted prices. Pat had pointed her in the direction of where it was parked. The clothes could be tried on at home provided you paid a deposit, or you could wait your turn in the queue outside a makeshift changing-room. Moira had her doubts about quality and choice, but found herself seduced by some smart combinations. She fell in love with a stylish one-piece outfit with a black, long-sleeved top and tartan skirt in red and black. So much for her desire for colour. A bright sapphire-blue, flowing top also caught her eye. Maybe she was still under the magical influence of springtime, even though late summer had arrived. Her number of garments grew to four. She would never have discovered clothing of this style in the department stores of London. Very chic. Her eyes were bigger than her pocket, but what a find.

"What a wonderful way to celebrate the arrival of a cheque," said Pat.

Scarlett met up with Moira. Charles was apparently having problems with Felicity over furniture ownership. Moira switched the conversation to her latest project, "I'm now looking to rent a small apartment."

"But why?" said Scarlett, knowing full well Moira had been having financial difficulties.

"Well, my superannuation cheque has arrived, so I feel I can afford to add some more comfort into my life. It's also about loving myself."

As Scarlett was driving them both back to West Gidding, Moira called out, "Stop!"

Scarlett braked as soon as she could and looked at Moira with surprise.

"I just saw a *To Let* sign. Let's go back and inspect the building," said Moira.

The property was in Main Street beyond the gallery and School of English. It was a Victorian building that had been divided into apartments. They knocked on the door. Of course, there was no answer, but Moira took the agent's details, hoping to ring at nine next morning. She returned to the cottage. She noticed the setting sun highlighting the street with a glow, and for the first time in a long time, she felt contented, and alive to the possibility that the future held new hope.

She rang Jack Smith, the estate agent, in the morning to check on availability.

"Would you have time to see it now?" asked the agent.

Moira glanced at her watch. "Yes of course."

It took him three minutes to drive her to the flat. The agent opened the solid oak front door with a deadlock key. There was a lounge to the left, opening out to the dining area and kitchen. The two bedrooms were on the right. Ironically, the light in the flat reminded her of the Sydney apartment, though the layout was different. She liked the idea of a second bedroom. It could double up as a guest room and studio. If her parents ever came to West Gidding, they would have somewhere to stay.

The walls had been recently painted white, and Moira liked the high ceilings. She would replace those pseudo paintings with originals. The carpets were worn in places, but nothing a colourful rug wouldn't cover. She also needed to buy some scatter cushions for the two-seater cream sofas.

A small-sized, established garden in front of the building was hers to care for. She liked the idea of planting some annuals; gardening would ground her. She had been through a lot in the last few months, and nest of her own would create some stability in her life.

Jack told her the tenant had left last weekend, so she could move in as soon as she signed a contract. She explained she needed to give Pat Myles at least one week's notice and asked Jack whether she could have a six months' contract with an option to renew it. They discussed further details and by then she was in no doubt that she wanted to live in this flat. It had been a long time since she felt so grounded and fulfilled. She slept well that night.

Next morning, while showering, she noticed marks all down on the right hand side of her body. She peered at them in the bathroom mirror. It was as if a set of long nails had scratched right down her torso. This puzzled her, as the right side was the side next to the wall where her single bed was placed. It would have been awkward for anyone to make the scratches on that side. So had Lady Penfold struck again? She really had let go of this ghost idea or she would send herself crazy.

Moira was ready to focus on her apartment move and set herself some tasks: to contact the agent to set up a contract signing time, and to collect cardboard boxes from the deli for the extra books and clothes that she had already managed to collect in such a short time. Just as well her tea chests hadn't arrived yet.

Tony had promised he would help her move the following Saturday, and was prepared to ferry her belongings and clothes in his car, taking several trips if need be. Pat was lending her some bedding until she was ready to purchase her own.

After her move, Moira gave herself space to enjoy her life again, as in walking in the *season of mists and mellow fruitfulness.* The spindly branches of the trees looked forlorn with the last of the leaves. Treating herself to a portable colour television, she watched documentary programs on the BBC. She spent time drawing and painting. Finally she received a letter to say her tea chests were docked in Southampton. She had fun exploring their contents when they arrived after clearing customs.

One day, while opening the front door to collect the milk bottles, she noticed that an envelope had been pushed through the letterbox. The writing looked familiar, her heart lurched as she opened it. Catching her breath, she saw a hand painted card, a cartoon of a woman moving into a new house with the words:

Happy Days in your New Home

All My Love

Mike

When they first met, Mike and she found a shared love of art: it had come late in both their lives, and had become a vehicle for personal change. On Leros they had strengthened their companionship with physical bonds of love. And now…?

Moira felt her eyes fill with tears, until the writing was so blurred she could not read it.

Then came the day when Moira had a call from Mike. The familiar butterfly movement in her stomach returned.

"I'm sorry to have been away for so long. I owe you an explanation. I need to speak to you urgently."

He had taken his time to contact her. Still, she had missed him.

"When?" she asked.

"Can I see you now?" he persisted.

Moira was startled by his serious manner. "I'm free now."

"I'll pick you up in twenty minutes."

Her imagination went into overdrive. Was he ill? Was he changing jobs? Was he moving to London? Was he bankrupt? And the question concerning her most – was he officially ending their relationship?

"Let's get out of West Gidding," he said abruptly on arrival.

They drove to a quiet pub on the way to Henfield. Moira remained silent. He ordered a pint of lager and she chose a lime and soda. She waited for him to begin. His facial muscles were taut.

"It's difficult to know where to begin," he said joining her at a table.

He placed his hands over her hands, as if supporting himself with her energy, and took a deep breath. He explained that some weeks before he had asked Moira to go to Leros with him, he had spoken to his lady friend, Margaret, whom he had been casually dating for six weeks. He told her that he believed honesty was the best way to go forward. Their relationship was at an end because he had fallen in love with a woman he had only met recently.

At first Margaret had asked him a few general questions, which he had answered.

"I regretted revealing I had fallen in love as soon as I had said so because of her subsequent reactions, said Mike."

Margaret accused him of leading her on into a relationship. He reminded her that he had been very explicit at the beginning of their dating. He was sorry if he had upset her but he had been clear. Then the shouting and foul language started for all to hear in the restaurant. Helpless in the face of her emotional reaction, he had said, "Let me take you home."

Her whining continued for the entire journey to her home. At one stage, he thought she would never get out of the car. When he arrived at his house, he phoned his doctor to check on her.

"When I returned from Leros, I found several hysterical messages left on my phone by Margaret. Then after two days, her doctor left a message asking me to contact him urgently."

Mike wiped his forehead with a handkerchief. "That's when I discovered that Margaret had attempted suicide. Luckily, she had been discovered by a friend early enough to be saved at the local hospital." He stopped to catch his breath. "I was horrified by the news," said Mike. "I tried to call you to share this unfortunate news on with you, but Pat said you had already left for Australia."

Moira felt numb, but was relieved he had come

clean with Margaret.

"Then the doctor advised me to involve myself in the counselling, which Margaret attended, as part of her process of letting me go."

At these words, Moira's heart sank. This could go on for months. She sympathised with Mike; it must have been a traumatic experience. On the other hand, she felt there was no place for a third person while Mike continued to be involved with Margaret's counselling. She was plunged into the void of uncertainty.

"So what happens next?" she said.

"I have to take part in this counselling, for as long as it takes, but this in no way changes what I feel for you and our growing relationship. Leros brought us together in a very special way and we have a lifetime ahead of us." His eyes pleaded with her.

Mike saw how pale Moira had grown; how her hands opened up with helpless gestures.

"Thank you for telling me all this. I appreciate your frankness," she said.

"I was concerned she may have tried to bother

or contact you in some way."

"No. But I need time to think about all this. I don't know if I can cope with this situation. I don't want to be responsible for a woman's suicide," she said.

"I'm the one who feels responsible for the suicide attempt. I'm the one who feels guilty."

He leaned forward, gazing intently into her eyes.

"We can still meet up, you know."

The quiver in his voice surely meant that he loved her.

"Just please take me home now."

He held her hand and tried to kiss her before she left his car, but she was already easing herself out and the kiss fell on her shoulder.

Moira pondered on Mike's revelations while tackling the domestic chores. The news had left her feeling shivery and cold; let down. She wondered whether Mike had continued to see Margaret at the same time as he dated her: then, she raced to the bathroom bringing up the contents of her stomach over the toilet bowl just in time. Overcome, she sought refuge in her bed.

In the morning, something which had been niggling at the back of her mind flashed to the forefront. The phone calls. The nuisance phone calls, which had been directed at her, must have been from Margaret. She had to tell Mike. His phone continued ringing but there was no answer.

Chapter 20

A few days later, Lady Allthorpe was on the phone.

"Hello Elizabeth. Did your friends like the painting you bought for them?"

"They were polite enough to say they did. I'm ringing to ask you over for lunch next week. I heard you were making enquiries at the Historical Society." The gossip grapevine again. "I believe I may be able to help you with your enquiries about the Penfolds. Did you know they were relatives of mine, in the sense that I married into the family?" Without waiting for a reply, she continued, "How is everything?"

"Slowly being sorted out. I assume your lunch is casual, Lady Allthorpe."

"Elizabeth please. I won't be wearing my ballgown, but not my jeans either. Don't worry about getting here. I will send my car and driver for you."

Moira had invited Zara to her new home. Moira was shocked to see that Zara's shoulders sagged, her wrinkles seemed to be more prominent, and she fidgeted with her hands more than usual. Moira wondered if she had judged her too harshly in the past.

"How are you, Zara?" Moira rested her hand on Zara's shoulder in sympathy without taking her eyes off Zara's face. "Scarlett told me Edward had created a scandal when he was involved in a murky shooting incident."

"It's all been too much," Zara whispered as she broke down in tears and stifled a sob. "There's more. I've never told you about the baby."

"What baby?"

"Some years ago Edward and I were lovers and I got pregnant. Edward didn't want the baby but I decided to have it." Zara broke down crying. "The baby was born prematurely so it needed extra care."

"I'm sorry to hear that."

"Edward had never worked, as his money was inherited, and he was irresponsible with how he spent it."

As her sniffling intensified, Moira handed over

a box of tissues.

"Edward was unreliable with his financial help. I had to find a job to cover basic costs of living. I worked at a waitressing job as well as in a pub."

"Who babysat your baby?"

"My mother was still alive and took care of Lucy. She enjoyed having her."

"My situation improved when I switched to working as a sales assistant in the fashion department of Selfridges. With time, I was promoted to the position of buyer, and continued with that for the next few years. I enjoyed the fashion side, and that position also opened up doors for running my own business in West Gidding when I was ready to start – the art gallery of course."

"Incredible."

"Leaving London was a good idea. I moved to Bramber, where I had a nanny. I wanted the gallery in a different village to Bramber and it took time to find."

Zara's voice had calmed down with the telling of the story. Her words were no longer a torrent of syllables.

Moira chewed over the implications of what she had heard. Zara was an amazing woman.

"Thank you for trusting me with your story. I suppose the gallery became your project?"

"Of course."

"And the fire not only hit you financially but it was like a sabotage of your entire creative output?"

"Yes. Edward was never interested in the baby but he seems to want to see Lucy more, now that she is a little girl. The trouble is he's unreliable with his fatherly responsibilities and that doesn't help Lucy or me. Also he's unstable emotionally."

"How old is your little girl?"

"Six years old."

"I'd love to meet her."

"I'm sure you will."

"So you protect Edward because he is Lucy's father?"

"Yes. But I didn't want to marry him and have to deal with his emotional eccentricities: it would have been draining. He often acts like a child, as if competing with Lucy for my attention. That was why he stole the mounted painting. Sometimes he is jealous of my success with the gallery, as if that overshadows his art, but I still don't believe he started the fire deliberately."

Another passenger in a relationship, thought Moira.

"If you ever need my help, don't hesitate to ask," she said.

Strange how West Gidding had brought together Zara, broken by her messy relationship with Edward, Felicity engrossed in the art world to the detriment of her own chances of having children, Moira herself, tainted by abuse in her marriage, and Scarlett, seeking a father as a partner. They were all damaged goods in one way or another. They all needed to learn to appreciate their own worth. Moira now understood that the ghost was the link between them all, the energy moving around the village.

Mike rang a few times, but Moira pleaded pressures at work. Her previously teeming emotions seemed to have been frozen. She wondered whether

Mike had been at fault with what he had offered Margaret; sometimes a man's body language could contradict the spoken word. Eventually she agreed to meet him for a coffee. He started filling her in on the counselling sessions.

"Stop. Let's talk about your painting? Are you painting or is that taking the back seat?"

"When would I have time to paint?"

"How is your work then?"

"Plenty of clients, except I can't seem to concentrate. Are you trying to make things difficult for me?"

"Why did you take Margaret to the barbecue when you had started dating me?"

"Shortly after speaking to her about breaking up, I received a phone call from Margaret, who was all charm this time. She said there was a barbecue at West Gidding for foreign students and locals. She suggested we go to it for old time's sake – as friends. I preferred peace to warring and decided to go along with her invitation. Later, I realised she had manipulated me."

Moira stared at Mike. She wanted to believe him.

"I never told her I was going to Leros on holiday with you."

Moira had started to get up, "I can't cope with all this. Don't ring me until you are free of counselling."

She stood up and strode purposefully out of the cafe.

The following week, Moira arrived at Lady Allthorpe's home and was shepherded into the conservatory. Elizabeth rose from her wicker chair to greet her, with a glass of chilled chardonnay. Moira had imagined a butler on the premises. Instead Elizabeth introduced her to Dolly, a homely housekeeper, who doubled up as cook and maid. Elizabeth registered Moira's surprise.

"These are difficult economic times," Elizabeth explained, with a wry half-smile.

Olives and cheese were set out on the glass table between their wicker chairs. A table had been set for lunch at the other end of the conservatory where they eventually sat down. Moira noticed how they faced a garden which had been allowed the freedom to spread its tentacles without being a wilderness.

Never reticent in what she had to say, Elizabeth began speaking about the Penfolds.

"I assume you already know the gist of Lady Penfold's story. What is less known is what happened to her lover."

Apparently Lady Penfold's lover had been falsely accused of stealing, and had been deported to Sydney in Australia. After serving his time, he moved to the city of Adelaide, a free settlement.

"Eventually he established vineyards, that became a successful commercial enterprise which following generations continued to manage," said Elizabeth.

Moira told her how her parents lived in South Australia.

"Yes Moira. Everything happens for a reason. You had to connect with Lady Penfold on an energetic level. She was an educated woman and healer, and vowed to help women who were abused or victimised."

Moira thought of the hotbed of troubled women in West Gidding: sexy dark haired ex-dancer, Scarlett; Yugoslav gallery owner, Zara, with dark secrets from the past; artist Felicity refusing to have children in order to carve out a career in a male-dominated art world; and herself, victim of abuse from her husband. All of them were breaking out from their shells, undergoing transformation and moving out of their fears, limitations and negative energies. Perhaps she was the only one who was conscious of this.

Elizabeth continued, "The ghost in your cottage is Lady Penfold. Her spirit would find no rest until women could increase their self-empowerment."

Moira had much to digest in the evening.

When Moira returned to the flat, another envelope was waiting for her. This time the hand-painted card was bigger, more colourful and more abstract.

I love you

I'm freed from the shackles of counselling.

Your Mike

When she viewed the front of the card again, Moira realised that it was a poetic invitation to return to Leros for *unfinished business* and to celebrate Mike's freedom. Moira smiled, her eyes lighting up. She wasn't sure what *unfinished business* referred to but she would find out.

The phone rang. It was probably Mike.

"Hello," said Moira.

"It's Guido," the voice whispered.

Moira felt a shooting pain in her stomach. Memories came at her in waves, making her feel nauseated. She felt as if her heart might burst through the paper walls of her chest.

"Hello?" the voice persisted.

Moira was too overwhelmed to respond.

"Just joking. It's Tony."

Moira was dumbfounded

"Moira, are you there? I'm so sorry," said Tony who was clearly worried he had pushed the trust boundaries too far.

Within seconds, Moira burst into peals of belly laughter that transformed themselves into hysterical giggles. She had travelled far in the last few months, in more ways than one. West Gidding was looking up, because she had chosen to see the miracle of life. Wounds had healed. She had been right. 1985 was a good year, even if it had started late.

"You're a devil, Tony," said Moira, "but you always make me laugh, thank you."

After chatting to Tony, Moira rang Mike.

"I would love to take up your offer to go to Leros again."

"We both need at least another week to renew our memories of it. Only this time I'm paying for both of us, so it's a suite where we have a king size bed to share."

"A king size bed," Moira sighed. "You'll have fun chasing me around that."

"Perhaps we should start practising now," said Mike.

"Why not? I've decided 1985 is my year after all."

"What about dinner tonight?"

"You're not wasting any time."

"I've had a difficult few months. I've much to catch up on."

Moira sensed the relief in Mike's voice.

"Can you be ready to leave to leave for Leros in two days' time?" said Mike, his voice as silky as when he first met her.

"Can I ever?"

What mattered was not what was lost in the past, but what existed in the present.

Moira's lesson during the year of changes had been to recognise the power of loving herself. Only then was she able to open her own heart to love others fully. Love was the energy that pushed the chess pieces over the board of life, opening one's heart to risks.

It was love that made the unpalatable, acrid experiences of the moment zing. Love brought out that giving side that was precariously balanced by selfishness. And yes, love came from the heart.

Further Reading

Thank you for taking the time to read this novel. If you enjoyed it, please tell your friends and post a review on Amazon.

Nonfiction by the same author:

Moving from Grief in Cornwall:
http://getbook.at/FCttA

South America Under the Skin of a Foreign Country:
http://bookShow.me/B00Y8SY57O

About the Author

Barbara M Webb has lived in seven of the fifty countries she has visited. She graduated with a B.A majoring in English at Queensland University, and she taught English in Australia and the UK. Writing has always been part of her life. When she isn't travelling, she lives between Cornwall and Quito in the Andes Mountains.

More about Barbara M Webb on her website and blog:
www.cornwall2theandes.com

Or follow her on twitter:
@cornwall2andes

69936815R00177

Made in the USA
Columbia, SC
30 April 2017